About

Having worked in the Civil Aviation scene for thirty-six years, Ron Wilkinson then embarked on a new career working on the UK's motorways. Now an accomplished author and model maker on the Royal Navy, he has won many accolades in these fields.

Beginning of the End

Ron Wilkinson

Beginning of the End

Vanguard Press

VANGUARD PAPERBACK

© Copyright 2025
Ron Wilkinson

The right of Ron Wilkinson to be identified as author of
this work has been asserted by him in accordance with the
Copyright, Designs and Patents Act 1988.

All Rights Reserved

No reproduction, copy or transmission of this publication
may be made without written permission.
No paragraph of this publication may be reproduced,
copied or transmitted save with the written permission of the publisher, or in
accordance with the provisions
of the Copyright Act 1956 (as amended).

Any person who commits any unauthorised act in relation to this publication
may be liable to criminal prosecution and civil claims for damages.

A CIP catalogue record for this title is available from the British Library.

ISBN 978-1-83794-392-0

This is a work of fiction. Names, characters, businesses, places, events and
incidents are either the products of the author's imagination or used in a
fictitious manner. Any resemblance to actual persons, living or dead, or actual
events is purely coincidental.

Vanguard Press is an imprint of
Pegasus Elliot Mackenzie Publishers Ltd.
www.pegasuspublishers.com

First Published in 2025

Vanguard Press
Sheraton House Castle Park
Cambridge England

Printed & Bound in Great Britain

Dedication

To my family and friends who have put up with a lot! Carol, David, Sam and Jessica. Alan, Sheila, Dave, Lyn, Jean Pierre, Janet. And Margaret. Also to many friends and workmates who have 'crossed the bar'. Alf Matley, George Faulkner, Len Potts. Frank Fitzgerald and others.

Acknowledgements

All the staff at Pegasus.

From the same author:

The Captain Alan Lee series
Book 1 In Our Darkest Hour
Book 2 The End Of The Beginning.
Book 3 The Beginning Of The End

Introduction

We continue the story of Captain Alan Lee R.N. We have moved on to late 1943/1944. Britain and her allies, after the setbacks of the previous years, are now building up their strength to go on the offensive.

Preston, his beloved first ship, is gone, but his new command *Stockport*, is building herself a strong reputation, strengthened by the loyal men who have transferred with him.

He is given a small squadron of aircraft carriers and his instructions are to return to the Far East and cause as much damage and destruction as possible to the Japanese forces. However, the losses he has suffered over the years are taking their toll.

First, we return to his exploits in WWI, as a very young Alan Lee serving onboard a Destroyer in the North Sea and the Dover Straights.

Zeebrugge

Late December 1916, Sub-Lt Alan Lee received his new orders, he was to proceed to Dover, to join the Tribal class Destroyer *Mohawk*, as her navigating officer, and he also received his other half stripe. Now officially Lieutenant Alan Lee R.N. So, it was with some sadness he left *Caroline*, leaving behind Captain Crooke, Lt. Vaughan and the rest of the ship's company. This would be a different kind of war, no more boring patrols finding nothing, with long days moored in windswept Scapa Flow.

In Dover Harbour, H.M.S. *Mohawk* left harbour every afternoon. She then spent the night patrolling the 'Dover Barrage', the line of nets, booms, and mine fields that stretched from the Kent beaches to the French coast, its function was to protect the troop convoys that came and went to France. They were also tasked to hunt for submarines entering and leaving their bases at Bruges, Ostende, and Zeebrugge, that were attempting to pass down the channel into the Atlantic, from there to attack the merchant shipping. Dark and brooding, the powerful German Destroyers were based in Zeebrugge and Ostende, who sailed daily to harass and attack the Trawlers and Drifters that monitored the 'barrage'. Another role they exploited with great efficiency was laying mines around the English Coastline, and when possible, to attack the poorly protected merchant shipping in the waters around the channel. This was *Mohawk*'s war, the cut and thrust of a short sharp engagement. As *Mohawk*'s new Navigator, Lee's skills would be severely tested, in the wreck and sandbank-strewn channel. The intense training under Vaughan, his previous navigator/trainer, held him in good stead, Goodson, the Captain of *Mohawk*, quickly realised that he had a very good officer, popular with his men, highly competent at his job, and a valued member of the wardroom.

They usually sailed around 1700 hours, darkened the ship, and left for one of the designated patrol lines. Early Jan 1917, *Mohawk* and her five sisters, sailed into a very dark night, with the wind rising and the temperature dropping like a stone. Information received from the Royal Navy Intelligence at Room 40, The Admiralty Building, had predicted that the Germans had planned a raid into the Dover Straights.

From the start, things did not go to plan for the British Destroyers, the force became split, and only *Mohawk*, *Tarter* and *Viking*, stayed together. Early the next day, they sighted ships in the distance, unsure if they were friend or foe, when *Viking* issued the standard identification challenge. The Germans responded by opening fire. *Mohawk* took multiple hits, she fell out of line, and her helm jammed. Lee was on the bridge, trying to keep track of their position, they were close to the shifting sands of the Goodwin Shoal. Hit by two shells on the bridge, the Captain and a signalman were injured, so Lee took command, and got the ship back under control. *Viking* was following, and almost ran into *Mohawk*; however, it did take some of the gunfire away from *Mohawk,* and onto *Viking*. The enemy retired, and *Tarter* took *Mohawk* in tow and towed her into Dover for repairs.

After temporary repairs, *Mohawk* left for refit at Chatham dockyard. This was the first leave, Lee had since the start of the war. He made his way home for the peace and quiet. Unfortunately, his mother had different ideas! Lee was dragged around various meetings for the WVRS, Woman's Institute, Church meetings and recruitment fetes, and other places. He was so happy when leave was over and he could return to his ship.

On return, the ship had altered a lot, gone were her 12pdrs main guns, they had been replaced by 4in Quick Firing guns, extra splinter shields had been worked into the bridge and other open positions, and the twin torpedo tubes had been updated to triple tubes, and a fresh coat of paint, the ship looked splendid. So, it was back to the usual old grind of patrols and short sharp actions. By late 1917, the food situation was becoming acute. So much merchant shipping was being sunk, that the severe rationing was taking a terrible toll on the civilian population. The Fleet suffered as badly as the population. In a desperate measure, the Naval food store at Deptford was opened and the contents were distributed to the fleet. When *Mohawk* received her quota, the oak casks were marked as sealed in 1805 and said to contain salted pork or beef. Unfortunately, those who had sealed the casks had supplied underweight and poor quality. The cooks onboard, reported that it was all probably salted horse meat. So heavily salted, that when *Mohawk* put to sea, the daily ration of meat was placed in a hessian sack and towed behind the ship, in an attempt to wash out the salt, thus making it more palatable.

Sat in the Wardroom, one evening, Lee spotted a notice from Dover Castle, asking for volunteers for a special action. He reached for a signal pad and started writing.

His application was accepted, and he was ordered to proceed to Portsmouth and report to Commander Roger Keyes. Lee's role was second in command of the old armoured cruiser *Thetis*, and her role was to be sunk in the canal that linked the U-boat base at Bruges with the port of Zeebrugge. The plan was to land Royal Marines on the mile-long mole at Zeebrugge, and suppress the gunners on the mole. Then sail in three block ships, *HMS*'s *Thetis, Intrepid* and *Iphigenia*, which were filled with concrete, and sink them in the canal entrance, thus bottling up the troublesome U-boats that were wreaking havoc amongst the merchant ships.

The failure of the Royal Marine assault on the Zeebrugge mole, caused by very heavy and accurate gunfire, decimated the Marines, causing many casualties. This resulted in the Germans being able to shift targets and concentrate their fire on the three blocking ships. *Thetis* did not make it to the canal entrance; as she approached the harbour, she hit an underwater obstruction and became stranded. Hit repeatedly, *Thetis* was soon a bloody shambles, dead and dying littered her decks. The noise was tremendous, as shell after shell pounded the wreck, the stench of cordite and explosives all-pervasive. Stacks of timber and splinter mats were on fire. The Captain and the Engineering Officer were killed, and this left Lee in command. Sheltering on the undamaged port side he ordered the remaining crew to abandon ship. The wounded was assisted by the able-bodied, these being passed down the barnacle-encrusted ships' side. Once he was happy there was no living left onboard, he slithered down the hull, lacerating his hands and feet on the hundreds of razor-sharp barnacles. On entering the freezing water and regaining his breath, he swam to the nearest raft and clambered aboard. Lee took command of the rafts and commenced the rescue of their shipmates. After which they awaited rescue by one of the escorting destroyers. Before abandoning the ship, it had settled on a sandbank, he had the scuttling charges fired, and these ripped out the bottom of the ship; it would be many years later when *Thetis* was finally removed.

Wet, bedraggled, covered in cuts and bruises, his uniform ripped and torn, he was landed at Dover docks. Here he was to await the return of *Mohawk*. He made his way to the Dover Court Hotel, where he commandeered a hotel room for a bath and something to eat. A bellboy was sent out to the nearest naval outfitters, where he returned with an oversized jacket; this would suffice till he returned to *Mohawk*. He sat down after his meal and fell fast asleep, the sleep of exhaustion. Later the bellboy awoke him to explain that *Mohawk* was just docking. The hotel management refused to accept payment, and with the bellboy by his side, carrying a great big food hamper for the ship's company, he rejoined his ship.

Much later he found out he had been awarded a Mention in Despatches for his action on *Thetis*, at Zeebrugge. This action left a deep impression on the young officer.

1 Home

The Sunderland Flying boat touched down in a flurry of noise and sea spray. It bounced momentarily from one wave top to the next, then settled in the water like a broody hen. It slowly wallows towards the jetty; eager hands are there to receive it. After a few moments as the ground crew secures the flying boat, the passengers are allowed to disembark. Lee was back home, the seaplane terminal in Southampton.

Captain Alan Lee RN, DSM, DSC, MiD, gets stiffly to his feet, it's been a long journey from Port "T" Britain's secret base in the Indian Ocean. He had left his ship *HMS Stockport*, refuelling in the harbour at Gan, and had been ordered to board a waiting aircraft for onward passage to the UK. His Executive Officer Andy Watson had orders to continue in command, and to take the ship to Durban, South Africa, for a much-needed refit. Lee had been ordered to London ASAP! So, he boarded an RAF-flown Liberator bomber, her name in large letters on her cockpit sides '*Thumper*', complete with a painted caricature of Disney's 'winged rabbit'. The aircraft had been crudely converted to carry 10 passengers. They were soon heading for Aden, it was a long, noisy, and uncomfortable trip. After landing for fuel at Aden, a quick walk to stretch the legs. They were airborne again, heading for Alexandria in

Egypt. Here they had to disembark and stay overnight, as the flight crew needed their rest period.

After a fitful night he was awoken by the night porter, and after a brief wash and shave he made his way to the hotel lobby to meet the rest of his travelling companions; they waited for an Army 3-ton truck to turn up and take them to the airfield. On arrival at the RAF Airfield, they found out that the aircraft had a technical issue, and they would be a couple of hours late in taking off. So, they all trouped back into the hut being used as a terminal and made themselves comfortable in the dusty and smoky building. Pestered by flies, lukewarm tea to drink, with stale sandwiches. Two hours later, it was a very relieved bunch of passengers, who reboarded the repaired aircraft. Moments later the heavily laden aircraft trundled down the runway and staggered into the air.

Lee sat opposite an Army Major, whom he recognized from the time his ship *Preston* had been evacuating troops from the island of Crete, the Major had been in command of one of the evacuated soldier regiments. He updated Lee on what was going on in the Mediterranean area of operations. He also hinted that there would be a major joint service 'undertaking' very shortly, and he was on his way to Gibraltar to finish off the details, all very 'cloak and dagger'. After cool lemonade was passed around the passengers, and with the steady thrum of noise from the four engines, Lee dozed off into a fitful sleep.

Suddenly, the aircraft pitched to port, as shouting and an increase in engine noise awoke Lee from his slumbers. He looked in amazement as a line of holes appeared in the fuselage roof, how odd he hadn't noticed them before! The Army Chaplin in the seat in front, slumped forward with blood erupting from a neck wound. The aircraft pitched to starboard, as the pilot was desperately trying the shake off their attacker. It then stood on its starboard wingtip as it clawed around to avoid another string of tracer bullets that streaked past the nose of the aircraft. People, luggage, papers, drinks etc., all flew across the inside of the fuselage. Lee could hear the groan from the airframe as it absorbed the g-forces inflicted on it. The engine noise had increased, and he could hear raised voices in the cockpit, but he was trapped in his seat by the force of gravity, so could not help. The aircraft levelled out, and Lee could hear the stutter of machine gun fire as the tail gunner tried to drive their attacker away. Being converted for passenger work, the aircraft had been stripped of the bulk of its defensive armaments, just the twin fifty calibres in the tail turret had remained. The pilot was desperately trying to keep the tail of the aircraft towards their attacker.

Major Hans Muller was sitting in the cockpit of his FW190 *Jabo* high over the Sicilian Narrows. The incessant sun beat down on his cockpit. He was tired, dog tired, he was flying on instincts now, his mind had difficulty focusing, he kept thinking back to his childhood; he and his brother Eric, playing in the hills and woods around their parents' home. He snapped back into reality; Eric had been lost in the first year of this damn war, lost when his submarine had been sunk by British warships, how he missed Eric. He, Hans, had started in the *Luftwaffe* as a Stuka pilot.

Seeing action, in Poland, Norway, France, and then down here in the Mediterranean, where he was the only survivor of his *Stuka* squadron. When it was realised how vulnerable the *Stuka* was, the squadron had converted to the Focke Wolf 190 fighter bomber. Now his second squadron had been decimated in the battles over North Africa in support of the *Afrika Korps*. It was clear the damn Tommies were getting the upper hand, gone are the days when the *Luftwaffe* ruled the skies. His head jerked forward, damn he was tired, time to return to the airfield in Sicily. He banked to his right. As he did so he spotted a flash from an aircraft windscreen. He turned towards it, ah! A Yankee B-24 Liberator bomber, crossing from his left to right, he headed to intercept, mindful of the heavy defensive armament it carried. He glanced at his fuel gauge, just enough petrol to attack this bomber and then home for a hot bath and bed. He lined up to make a forward slashing attack, knowing that the B-24 was vulnerable to head-on attacks. He pitched down and as the bomber filled his gun sight, he pressed the firing button.

The aircraft had been cruising along at 9,000 feet towards Gibraltar, passing through the air gap between Cape Bon and Sicily. When they were spotted by a prowling German FW190. The B-24 flight crew were in a lethargic mood and had not spotted the lone German fighter until it was too late. A twenty mm cannon shell exploded in the radio compartment, as a line of thirteen mm machine gun bullets tore into the fuselage. The rear gunner was trying desperately to find their attacker, his fingers caressing the firing buttons. The B-24 dived towards the sea, finally levelled out at 100 feet above the water, the pilot remembering his training 'lower is best'. The Fw190 slid into the range of the tail gunner, who let fly with his weapons.

Muller, lined up on the rear gunner, had to shut him down. As he concentrated on a deflection shot, he felt his aircraft stagger as machine gun bullets stitched across his left wing! 'Damn, I'm hit,' he thought.

Sergeant Eddie Moss, the tail gunner, watched as the Nazi aircraft got closer, waiting, waiting, he started firing, his tracer rounds heading towards their attacker. He watched as sparks flew from the aircraft wing, yeah got him! The German fighter reared up and headed towards Sicily with smoke pouring from its wing.

Muller rolled to his right, his fighter sluggish to the controls. 'Time for home,' he thought. Twenty minutes later he lined up for his landing, glancing at his fuel gauge, it was empty. After touch down, just as he turned towards the hanger, his engine stopped, out of fuel. He staggered from his aircraft exhausted. His ground crew helped him to his room, and his servant helped him into his bunk.

Onboard the Liberator, chaos reigned, blood and gore were everywhere, leaking fuel and hydraulic oil were swilling around under the aircraft keel plates. The radio room was destroyed, the remains of the Radio Operator and Navigator plastered the walls and bulkhead, killed instantly. Number 2 port inboard engine was on fire, and the co-pilot was wounded, but incredibly the pilot was uninjured. Due to good fortune, a doctor had boarded at the last minute, and he immediately set about attending to the wounded. Along with the two dead crew members, two civilian scientists and the Army Vicar had also been killed, and there were also injuries to two other staff officers. The pilot and co-pilot managed to extinguish the engine fire, gain height and continue towards Gibraltar. Moss, the tail gunner, with Lee and the Army Major, started clearing up the mess. Any unwanted items were thrown overboard to lighten the bomber, as it struggled to gain height. With no radio and no charts, they limped on, nobody aware of their plight.

Just as daylight started to fade, Gibraltar came into view. The Pilot skilfully lined the aircraft up with the runway, but due to some handling issues, he had to overfly part of Spain, which would bring howls of protest from the Spanish! Firing red lights, the universal signal that an aircraft was in trouble, the badly damaged B-24 made an isometric landing at the very Western end of the runway, and halfway down the runway, the undercarriage collapsed, and it slithered over to the Spanish side of the runway stopping about fifty feet short of the border. The Spanish border guards scattered as the errant damaged bomber headed towards them! Everybody onboard made a rapid exit, as the plane became enveloped in fire.

After being checked out by the medical team in the naval hospital, Lee was taken to a room in Admiralty House to rest and recover before his ongoing journey. The following day, he was taken down to the Destroyer pens, where a launch was waiting to take him out to a waiting Sunderland Flying boat. Once onboard, it commenced its take-off run, keeping well to the east of Algeciras Bay, so as not to provoke more protests from the Spanish. It climbed steadily and turned right to exit the Mediterranean Sea and then headed north for home.

Across the bay in Algeciras, enemy eyes were watching, as Lee and the others boarded the aircraft. A message flew across the ether, "VIPs in Sunderland heading north". The message was received at '*The Abwehr*', the German military intelligence headquarters, at 76/78 Tirpitzufer, Berlin, adjacent to the offices of the OKW.

Tired and still sore, Alan Lee slept for most of the journey home. Little did he know that a Ju88 fighter had been ordered from an airfield at Landivisiau, Brittany, France, to intercept and shoot down his aircraft. The Junkers aircraft had crashed on take-off, due to the fuel line being cut. Later, a member of the French Resistance and his family were executed for attempted sabotage.

2 New orders

Sir Dudley Pound sat in his office chair, his Chief of Staff stood by his side, and across from them sat Lee. On the table were charts, ledgers, signal pads, written messages, etc. A very pretty Second Officer Wren was sat to the side taking notes. The First Sea Lord spoke, "Captain Lee, thank you for attending, I am led to believe your journey here was a bit fraught?"

"Yes, sir, it was a bit exciting," replied Lee.

"Glad you are safe."

Lee thought, 'I might be, but some good men died in that plane crash!'

"Now, first congratulations on your command of Force 'Y', you really stuck it to the Japs! Shame about your losses, but no blame is being attached to you over them."

"Thank you, sir, they were great ships and airmen, they are a painful loss," replied Lee.

"Right, I have another Task Force for you if you want it?"

Lee was shocked. "Er yes sir, if you want me."

"Excellent, we are giving you a carrier task force, 4 carriers and enough suitable escorts, we have some work for you in Europe, then later the Far East, maybe, your full orders will follow!"

Lee was stunned. "Thank you, sir," was all he could say.

"First, you leave for the USA in four days' time, I want you to take some top secret papers to the 'Pentagon' in Washington, the contents don't need to concern you, but you must hand them to Admiral King, personally, in the US Navy department, then take a few days leave and then report back to your ship, OK, that's the business out of the way, you are being promoted to Commodore, you can choose your own flag ship from your force".

The Chief of Staff went through the force that Lee was to command, this would be known as the 30th Aircraft Carrier Squadron. It consisted of 4 American-made Escort Carriers, HMS's *Striker*, *Ruler*, *Fen*cer and the Canadian *HMCS Nabob*. In American parlance *CVE*, which stood for *A*ircraft *C*arrier *E*scort. The sailors in the Royal Navy had soon changed that designation too – *Cheap, Vulnerable, Expendable*! The light cruiser *HMS Bristol*, the Dido class AA cruisers *Diadem*, *Black Prince*, and *Cleopatra*. Plus, the Destroyers from the 26th Destroyer Flotilla *Savage, Stinger, Scorpion, Swift, Napier, Nepal*, The Norwegian *Stord* and finally the Dutch warship, *Van Galen*. All new warships that had powerful anti-aircraft armaments. He also had a small fleet train, with their own escort, he would join up with them later. He would travel to Portsmouth, where *Bristol* had just finished a refit and work up, so was ready for sea. Onboard, the 'X' turret had been removed, and replaced by a twin 4in mounting, and an 8-barreled Pom-Pom fitted, giving the ship impressive

AA firepower. All the other ships were on their way or already at Scapa Flow, awaiting his arrival.

The Chief of Staff, spoke, "OK, best uniform for tomorrow, you will be presented to the King, for your previous medals and we are giving you another DSC for your actions with that Jap cruiser force." Lee just sat there with his mouth open.

The Chief of Staff spoke again, "We have taken the liberty of contacting your wife, she is on her way here by train as we speak, there is a room booked at Claridge's for you both, and a car will pick you up at 11 o'clock sharp, don't be late! The day after tomorrow, report here at 9 for a full briefing on your new role, also nip into 'Gieves' and see if they can do a quick Commodore's uniform".

Lee stood and left the building, he was in a state of shock, he fully expected a dressing down for the loss of his ships, but instead, he had been promoted! He wanders to the front of the Admiralty building his mind in a daze, another pretty Wren was standing by a staff car awaiting him.

"Excuse me, are you Commodore Lee?" she asked.

He took a moment to acknowledge she was talking to him! He just nodded, not trusting himself to speak.

"This way, sir." She led him to the car. "Sir, I am Natalie, I am your driver, I have been assigned to you."

The next three days passed in a blur. Gieves managed to rustle up a jacket for the award ceremony, then delivered two magnificent dress uniform jackets adorned with the broad gold strip of a Commodore. The King was most kind, and being a sailor himself, was very interested in

Lee's last trip, he said he had been following his career with interest. Sheila, his wife, was over the moon with delight, staying at Claridge's, and having been invited to the ceremony at Buckingham Palace. His meeting with the Chief of Staff, however, was overshadowed by the news that Admiral Pound was unwell and did not attend the meeting. It was found out later he had a brain tumour and did not have long to live.

After making sure his wife Sheila was safely onboard the Plymouth bound train, Natalie, Lee's Wren driver, commenced their journey to join the Sunderland flying boat, complete with a heavy sealed briefcase, which was berthed in the Southampton waters, Then, it was a long tiring journey, first to the Azores to refuel, then onto Bermuda, for an overnight rest. Then finally alighting in the great harbour of New York, landing in the East River and then taxing to the seaplane terminal. There, a Cadillac saloon car awaited with two US Navy sailors, armed with sidearms, met him as he came ashore, and whisked him at high speed, to the Pentagon in Washington. On arrival, he was very impressed with the brand new building, and the fact that all the US armed services were under one roof, which seemed to Lee to be a great idea! He was ushered into a huge waiting area. Presently, Admiral King and his entourage arrived. Although reported as an ardent anglophobic, he greeted Lee with utmost courtesy, spent a short time in pleasant conversation, and then, briefcase in hand, left the room.

His two escorting sailors then asked him where he wanted to be taken. On a whim, he asked if he could be taken to New Jersey, where he had met the fantastic family, of Bill and Mona Crean, who had adopted him, when he was standing by *Preston* while she was being repaired. Here he was able to relax, talk about local issues, forget the war for a bit, and accept their hospitality. They even went up to New York, to watch a show on Broadway. All too soon, he had to make his way to the seaplane terminal, for his flight home. With a lump in his throat, he said good-bye to his American friends and boarded the Pan Am flying boat for his journey back to the UK. Fortunately, the Flying boat was a lot more luxurious than the outbound Sunderland, and he felt more rested and relaxed when they landed in Plymouth Harbour.

He was very surprised to see Natalie, his driver, waiting for him. A quick call at home for some clean clothes, then off they drove down the A38 towards his new command at Portsmouth. Weaving expertly through the endless convoys of army lorries, and five hours later they arrived at the Victory Gate. After the inevitable security check, he was waved through, towards Fountain Road Jetty, where *Bristol* awaited. After stepping out of the staff car he stood for a moment, looking at the ship, built in Swan Hunter's yard in Newcastle; she was a mirror image of his beloved *Preston.* All the memories came flooding back. He turned and thanked Natalie for her help over the past few days. A leading seaman was removing his luggage from the boot of the staff car, and as he walked up the gangway, a bosuns call went out, a Guard of Honour was called to attention, and as Lee saluted the quarterdeck, with a crack his broad pendant unfurled from the mainmast. Lee had joined his latest ship.

Stepping forward with his hand extended was his old executive officer, now, Commander Alf Matley RN. A welcome face amongst so many new ones!

"Welcome aboard *Bristol*, sir. Would you please inspect the Guard?" Matley asked.

"It would be my pleasure, Commander," replied Lee.

A short walk down the ranks of The Royal Marines, all resplendent in fresh Blanco, and boot polish. Lee stopped short.

"Hello, Marine Bennett, nice to have you onboard."

Bennett smiled. "Thank you, sir."

Lee also smiled, Bennett had served on his last two ships, a good solid reliable Marine onboard, but a rascal on shore leave!

"Thank you, Commander, an excellent turnout, despite the scoundrels onboard!"

This brought smiles from the side party.

"Please dismiss the men."

In a loud voice, Matley spoke, "OOW dismiss the men." Then to Lee, "Can I show you to your cabin, sir?"

Lee nodded.

Once Lee was in the cabin, they could dispense with formalities, they shook hands warmly,

"Alf, how pleased I am to see you again, tell me all that's been going on?"

"Sir, I have another surprise for you. Steward, bring in Commodore Lee's drink."

"Timmins! How wonderful, I last saw you in Portsmouth when we brought back *Wilton*." Timmins had been his steward onboard *Preston* until it had been sunk in the dark days in the Mediterranean.

"I am fine now, sir, a few weeks sick leave and I am back, I hope it was all OK I asked for this posting when I found out you were to take command."

"Of course, very pleased to have you around again."

Lee and Matley sat for a couple of hours talking 'shop' and old friends, Timmins supplied them with drinks and a snack. Then they discussed their orders and what the future held. The telephone rang, and Timmins answered, "Captain to the bridge sir."

Lee and Matley both jumped up and said in unison "on my way". They both stopped and all three burst into laughter.

"I guess I will have to get used to this!" said Lee as Matley left the cabin.

On the bridge everybody was looking overboard into the harbour, two of *Bristol*'s sailors had fallen from a work platform and ended up in the fast-flowing waters, the tide was on the ebb, so they were rapidly being taken out to sea. A lifebelt had been thrown, and one of the men had grabbed it and hung on. The second sailor was a poor swimmer and was clearly struggling in the cold water. The duty motor launch had been summoned but would take time to get to the scene. Berthed just ahead of *Bristol*, at the Gun Wharfe Quay, was the regular Isle of Wight ferry, *Ventnor*; onboard, able seaman Steve Wenham had spotted the unfolding drama. Stripping off his heavy watchkeeping coat and his seaboots, he grabbed a rope, tied it around his waist and waited for the fallen sailor to get closer. When close enough, he jumped overboard; the cold hit him like a sledgehammer, he struggled to breathe, his cork life vest brought him to the surface, and he struck out with a powerful breaststroke, and he managed to grab the errant matelot.

Keeping the struggling man afloat, Steve got a loop of rope around them both, to stop them drifting away. The duty launch appeared above them as four powerful hands hauled them unceremoniously aboard. Rough woollen blankets were wrapped around them as the launch headed a full speed for *Bristol*. All three men were aided in clambering up the gangway. They were taken down to sick bay, for the surgeon to have a look at them; there their wet clothes were taken away and all three were given hot showers and a tot of rum to warm them up. Matley came down to see them and was grateful to Steve for his efforts in rescuing his crewmen. He promised to replace his sodden clothing with clothes from 'The Slop Chest' and would write a thank you note to the Chairman of the Ferry Company and the Skipper of the *Ventnor*.

3 Scapa Flow

The Tannoy shrilled, "Hands for leaving harbour, Special Sea Duty Men close-up, second-degree readiness." They sailed with the tide. Two coal-fired paddle wheel tugs pulled and fussed to get *Bristol* clear of the jetty, their stocky funnels belching out black smoke, which left a sooty deposit on *Bristol*'s freshly painted upperworks, which really upset the Executive officer. Passing down the harbour, dodging the local harbour traffic and ferries, saluting Admiralty House, and out through the boom at the Round Tower, they followed the Local Escort Force Corvettes, as they hunted for any German U -Boats that may be lurking. A few families were gathered on Southsea Common to wave goodbye. Lee desperately hoped he could bring all his crews home safe. The passing ferry *Ventnor* flashed a message of 'good luck, and good hunting'. Passing the Palmerston Forts, then out into the channel, they thanked the L.E.F. for their help and they turned west and increased speed to twenty-five knots for Lands' End and then up the Irish Sea, and then Scapa Flow, base of the Home Fleet.

As they neared The Lizard, the radar room shouted up, "Radar...Bridge, two aircraft coming straight at us from the South, Green 90, range twenty-five miles".

Matley shouted, "Action stations."

The alarm rattlers sounded, followed by a stampede of seaboots, as ratings rushed to their action stations, pulling on lifejackets and anti-flash gear as they went.

"DCT...Bridge, I can see a Wellington bomber, trailing smoke from one engine, being chased by what looks like a Ju88 fighter."

The Captain replied, "Guns, very good, try to open fire on the Jerry as soon as you can."

Lee had come on the bridge and could just make out the wounded aircraft as it flew near to the surface of the sea, the enemy aircraft was weaving around behind it trying to get a shot in.

"DCT...Bridge, permission to open fire?" Matley looked across at Lee, who nodded.

"Open fire!" shouted Matley. The ship shuddered as her portside four-inch high-angle guns belched fire and smoke at the enemy. The familiar smell of cordite drifted across the upper bridge. Crack, the guns fired again.

Onboard Vickers Wellington 'P for Peter', the pilot was struggling with his controls. The German fighter had caught them unawares. They had just dropped their string of depth bombs on a U-boat periscope, and they were all watching for any signs of damage. The Jerry had dived down on them after hiding in a large cloud bank. The tail gunner had yelled out a warning but it had been too late. The port engine was on fire, and the pilot had shrapnel wounds in his left leg. He had spotted the two-funnel cruiser in the distance so knew it was friendly, and had headed towards it, keeping as low to the sea as possible. The Ju 88 was weaving about trying to get a firing solution, but the tail gunner was doing a great job of keeping him away. The German pilot managed to get a final burst of canon fire away, just as two of *Bristol*'s four-inch shells exploded on either side of his aircraft. His aircraft dived into the cold restless sea, there was no survivors. 'P for Peter' was doomed, her port wing dropped and the wingtip struck the sea, the aircraft cartwheeled across the ocean before landing on its back and started to slowly sink. *Bristol* headed towards the Wellington crash site, but there were no survivors. It did not become known till months later, 'P for Peter' had managed a textbook attack, that had straddled U-1012, which it sent to the seabed with all hands. A subdued ships company headed North for the Irish Sea.

It had been many months since Lee had last been in Scapa Flow, and he was surprised at the transformation. Many more gun batteries were visible around the Flow. A lot of new types of warships were going about their business – Battleships, Carriers, Cruisers, Destroyers, Escort ships of all shapes and sizes, a floating dock, repair ships, concert ship, and a small merchant ship, converted to brew beer for the fleet. The Fleet Base at Lyness had grown substantially, with Fleet Canteen, sports fields, golf course, and new fuel tanks. Some things never change, Admiral Jellicoe's flagship from Jutland, now the Fleet Flagship *Iron Duke*, was still sat on the mud where she had been beached to save her from sinking. From her signal bridge, the signal lamp flashed away "Commodore to repair onboard!"

On a bitterly cold and windy afternoon, *Bristol*'s barge nudged against *Iron Duke*'s companionway, as the barge crew held it steady, Lee, followed by Matley, stepped across and ascended the stairs. As his cap became visible, the warship side party came to attention and a bosun's call sounded. Commodore Lee had boarded the Fleet Flagship. Admiral of the Fleet Sir Andrew Cunningham, (universally known as ABC to the Fleet) stepped forward and accepted Lee's salute. Hand outstretched, he spoke, "Hello, Alan, how nice to see you again."

"Thank you, sir, it's been a long time."

"Right, come below out of this damn wind and tell me all about sinking Jap ships!" Lee had served under ABC in the dark days of the war in the Mediterranean when the German Luftwaffe very nearly broke the back of the Royal Navy. So many ships had been sunk or badly damaged during the evacuation of mainland Greece and the island of Crete, in an ill-founded operation that Churchill had insisted on. At one stage, Lee's *Preston* was the only cruiser available in the Eastern Mediterranean. Sat at Jellicoe's dining table, Lee, Matley, ABC, his Chief of staff and Flag Lieutenant sat down for some lunch. After which they had a friendly discussion about Lee's escapades in the Dutch East Indies. After half an hour it was down to business. "OK, Alan, this is what the Admiralty has in mind for your force. In one week's time, you will sail with your force to a position here!" He pointed to a spot on a chart just of the Norwegian coast. "There you will launch a full strike against the *Tirpitz*, she is held up in Kaa fjord, here." Again, he pointed to the map. "The carriers have been practicing for weeks now, so should be ready. The 'Beast' was attacked by our X-craft submarines and she had been badly damaged, but they have managed to repair her, so we need her knocked out, with the second front nearly upon us we need this ship sunk!"

"That's part one!" He continued, "Part two, with the successful landings in North Africa and Sicily, you are to enter the Eastern Mediterranean and attack enemy forces and shipping in and around the Ionian Sea, Adriatic and the Aegean Sea."

Lee was trying to take in the first part of the operation. Lee thought, 'Wow, a proper Cook's tour.'

The Admiral continued, "You may have noticed your force is not here, we know there is a German spy operating in the Islands until we catch the bugger, we wanted to keep your force well hidden, it's waiting for you at Loch Ewe." For the next few hours, all manner of operational matters was discussed. It was a very subdued but excited Lee that returned to *Bristol*. So much to plan for.

At five o'clock the following morning, yet again, the Tannoy sprang into life, "Special sea duty men close up, hands for leaving harbour, set defense watches." *Bristol* and Lee were going back to action.

At an airfield in Stavanger in Norway, behind a huge screen that had been erected in the space between three aircraft hangers, twelve of Germany's latest secret weapons, '*Mistel*', were being feverously worked on by dozens of black overall-clad mechanics. The aircraft had the nickname of 'Daddy and Son' or 'Piggyback'. It consisted of an unmanned 'War Weary' Ju88, armed with a shaped charge and packed with three-thousand-and-five-hundred kilograms of high explosives, and sitting on top, was a Fw 190 fighter. The idea was the combination would launch under the control of the fighter pilot. It then headed towards its target. On reaching the vicinity of the target, the fighter would detach the bomber, and then guide it by remote control to its destination. Developed in total secrecy by the German Air Ministry, and test flown by KG200 the *Luftwaffe* secret test squadron. This would be its first deployment as a weapon system. Flown overnight from Peenemunde in Germany, and then hidden when they landed in Stavanger. Prepared during the day, the crews were rested and briefed on their target. The British Home Fleet in Scapa Flow. The crews were woken at two o'clock in the morning, they hoped to reach Scapa as the dawn broke and catch the Tommies still asleep. As the pilots mounted their aircraft, they climbed a rickety ladder up to the FW 190 cockpit. In the darkness, there was a scream and a loud thud, one of the ladders had snapped, and the unfortunate pilot fell twenty feet to the ground, receiving serious injuries. So now there were eleven. At the set time, thirty-two engines coughed into life, one would not start! Now there were ten. From the control tower a red light flashed and ten aircrafts moved forward, taxing towards the runway. Aircraft number five, just as it taxied forward, lurched to the left, the starboard undercarriage had sunk up to its axle in the soft ground and twisted the aircraft around. So now there were nine. A green light flashed from the control tower; with a mighty roar, the first aircraft began its take-off roll. Once airborne, they formed up over the airfield, where their escort fighters joined them, again Fw 190s and Me 410s. They were late. Half an hour into the flight, aircraft number three had to abort; the pilot was unable to arm the bomb in his Junkers. Now there were eight. The sun came up and they were still thirty minutes away from Scapa. There was a heated discussion between the pilots as to whether they should abort the mission. However, it was decided to continue.

In the Orkneys, the radar stations on Hoy and the radar station at Wick in Scotland picked up the approaching German raiders and the alert was sounded. First, RAF Spitfires, scrambled from the airfield at Wick, and as they gained height, they headed out to intercept the enemy. Then from the runways of the Royal Naval Air Stations on the Orkneys, Hatston and Twatt, Sea Hurricanes, Martlets and Hellcats, leapt, snarling into the air, as they clawed upwards to gain height. They then tore across the Flow; a couple of the pilots noticed a *Town* class cruiser just moving down the Flow towards the boom gate.

The RAF Spitfires fell on the German escort fighter aircraft first, who were trying desperately to protect their charges. When the Spitfires disengaged, three Spitfires had fallen into the cold North Sea. Two Me 410s also crashed into the sea, followed by three Fw 190s and two *Mistel* combinations, this then left six. The escorting fighters had no sooner caught their breath when the Royal Navy fighters attacked. In the swirling dogfight, the *Mistel*'s pilots had to concentrate on their targets. The first combination, aimed at the Battleship *Relentless*. As the pilot released his bomber, he felt his fighter leap upwards, as it lost the 'dead weight'. He concentrated on guiding his bomber towards its target. Seconds later his aircraft was shredded by cannon fire from a Sea Hurricane, this severed the radio control of the bomber, which lurched to the right and smashed into the thick armoured belt of *Relentless*. Although it missed the weaker armour on the deck, it did cause extensive damage to the ship. Rapid and efficient damage control, saved the ship, but she would never sail again. The stricken fighter crashed into the sea next to his target. Another *Mistel*, headed towards the Escort Aircraft Carrier, *Streaker*, currently being used as an aircraft transport. She was loaded with brand new Avenger and Corsair aircraft and a flight deck full of Catalina flying boats. The bomber worked as advertised, and plunged straight into the tightly packed flight deck, there was a terrific explosion and *Streaker* disintegrated! However, the *Mistel* pilot did not live to enjoy his victory as gunfire from a Hellcat ripped his aircraft apart.

One headed towards *Bristol* with the intension of sinking her in the entrance of the Flow and blocking it. However, *Bristol*'s Gunnery Officer had different ideas, and the *Mistel* was hit repeatedly by the terrific barrage put up by the gun crews. Of the remaining attackers, one crashed on Longhope, one aircraft failed to separate and the combination crashed into a pair of Hunt class destroyers tied up at a buoy, sinking both. The last one exploded in a huge fireball as it tried to escape, and another five of the escort fighters also failed to return to Norway.

4 Loch Ewe

As *Bristol* cleared the Hoxa Gate boom, her crew was stood down from action stations and started clearing up the spent cartridge cases. She headed west into the Pentland Firth and started to roll badly, the sea was particularly bad, and wave height was eight to ten feet, which caused the big cruiser to shoulder her way to the southwest. Two friendly fighters circled overhead as an escort. A few hours later, as the daylight started to fade, they passed the boom defense vessel *Bargate* and entered Loch Ewe. Lee was stood on the bridge and was watching his new command coming into view. The whole force looked smart and efficient.

Lee spoke, "Captain, could you ask your Chief Yeoman to send a signal to all ships Captains to repair onboard *Bristol* at 1000 hours tomorrow, along with the Senior Pilots of the Carriers."

"Bunts make it so!" Matley spoke. In a quiet voice, "Sir, for operational messages please speak to the Yeomen direct, that will help you speed things up, and I am happy with that!"

Lee smiled, "Thanks, Alf, just trying to follow protocol."

Bristol came to a stop in the centre of the Loch Ewe, also known as Port 'A', in a vain attempt to fool the

German Intelligence, and anchored, snug and safe. The weather outside the sheltered Loch turned bad with the seas rising and the wind howled. Lee turned into his bunk, content with somebody else worrying about the safety of the ship.

The following morning the weather was blowing a full gale, some of the ships' Captains had a very wet and uncomfortable trip to the Flagship. They all assembled in the Wardroom as Lee's cabin was not big enough for the assembled numbers. Tea and coffee were served, and the cooks had laid on snacks. The pantry had been cleared of cooks and stewards, and armed Royal Marine sentries had been posted. Lee was an avid non-smoker but allowed them to smoke before the meeting started. Lee entered with Matley and gestured for everybody to sit down. He looked around and smiled at a few familiar faces, Dave Wilkinson, Mark Beddall, had served with him before, along with a few old shipmates.

Lee stood. "Gentlemen, good morning, welcome onboard. Most of you know each other, but may I introduce, *Nabob*, Cdr Jeremy Naismith, Royal Canadian Navy, *Stord*, Lt Cdr Stig Holsman of the Norwegian Navy, and finally, *Van Galen*, Cdr. Johan van Gelder of the Dutch Navy. May I say how pleased we have you here with us!" A round of applause went round the cabin. "Have you all got tea or coffee, and been to The Heads?" Laughter lit the room! "Very well, if you have not been told, you are now part of The 30th Aircraft Carrier Squadron! Our first mission will be an attack on the German Battleship *Tirpitz*!" An audible murmur arose. "We sail in two days' time, make sure you have all spares and equipment loaded, if not draw it from the store ship berthed here, and all fuel bunkers topped off. Once we have completed this mission, we will be sailing for the Med. Our presence is needed there. Questions?" The usual round of timings, bunkering, victuals etc. went on for the next hour. "Ok, have some lunch, then return to your commands, *Fencer*, *Ruler*, *Striker* and *Nabob* and Senior Pilots (known as SPLOTS) stay behind," After a pleasant hour over lunch, all the Captains got to know each other, and then a happy bunch of sailors returned to their ships.

After the other Captains had left, the Carrier Captains and their Senior Pilots gathered around the large mess table. "OK gentlemen, settle down, how are your aircraft crews getting on, what are your new aircraft like, is there anything I need to know about? *Ruler*, Mark, nice to see you again, you first." Cdr. Mark Beddall had been Lee's Gunnery office onboard *Preston*.

"Hello, sir, we have thirty aircraft onboard, fifteen Grumman Hellcats and fifteen Avenger bombers, good pilots and terrific aircraft".

Lee said, "Thanks, Mark, I had experience with both in the East Indies. What disciplines have they been practicing?"

"Sir, level bombing and torpedo attack."

"Very good, *Striker*, Dave, great to see you again, glad you have recovered from the Far East escapade!" Cdr Dave Wilkinson had served under Lee in command of a Cruiser, *Bellona*.

"Hello, sir, yes, the same as *Ruler*, I have fifteen Hellcats and fifteen Avengers. The Avengers and the Hellcats have specialized in dive bombing and Avengers also in torpedo attack.

"Great, Dave, thanks."

"*Nabob*, Jerry how are things?"

"Thank you, sir, we also have thirty aircrafts, the same as the others. Fifteen Hellcats and fourteen Avengers, we lost one a few days ago, but a crew has been dispatched to Hatston for a replacement. They have been practicing all disciplines, and I am happy they can be efficient at them all."

"Thanks, Jerry, can I ask where the ships name comes from?"

"Sir I have been told it's a Muslim word for the Mongols."

"Ah! thanks." Smiles all round.

"And last but not least, *Fencer*, Captain George Metcalf RN. Hello, George, it's been a long time since that old stuffy office in the Admiralty building!"

Metcalf smiled. "Yes, sir, glad we are not still there! We have fifteen Seafires, lovely looking aircraft, but short of range and very fragile when deck landing, we have had a lot of replacement aircraft during training. Also, we have twelve Fairy Barracudas, the lads call them Flying Christmas Trees, so much equipment has been put onboard, they are dreadfully slow and underpowered, but they are an effective torpedo bomber."

"OK, thanks for your input." Lee looked at Mark Beddall's SPLOT. "Lt Cdr Miles Davies, you are the most senior pilot here. I am therefore making you the 30th Aircraft Carrier Squadron Air Wing Commander, you will be responsible for all operational planning, replacement crew, and aircraft, you will deal with me, all you other pilots will raise any issues etc. with Miles, who will forward them on to me, understood?" Nods all round. "Also, you don't need to ask me for everyday issues and flying, you deal with them. OK?"

"Yes, sir, understood."

Lee spoke again, "SPLOT, any issues you want to raise?"

"Yes, sir, there is one I need to make you aware of, The Avengers we have onboard are two different marks, one and two. They are built by two different companies, and there is a marked difference in their performance, finish, parts, etc., the engineers are struggling with getting appropriate spare parts etc. for the aircraft, we may have some issues later on, but I will keep you informed."

"Very well, keep me updated and I will shake a few trees!"

"OK, so then there's no need for additional signaling when routine flying is taking place, takes the pressure of the Bunting Tossers," Lee continued. "Right, the target is the *Tirpitz*," an audible sigh went around the table, "she is here berthed in Kaa Fjord, that folder," pointing at a large well-stuffed manila folder, "contains all the intelligence info, and photos we have. OK, Senior Pilots, take it with you, go and discuss what you want to do, be back here at 1000 hours tomorrow, I want to see a strike plan.

Dismissed." They stood and left the wardroom to return to their ships.

The next day, the Senior Pilot, Miles Davies, along with the other senior pilots, came back aboard. "Sir, we have a plan here for your inspection, based on intelligence from N.I.C. the Norwegian underground and RAF photos."

"Go ahead," relied Lee. Davies laid out a map of Northern Norway on the table and placed his notepad next to it. "This is what we came up with, all the information for the strike came from the latest info from the Admiralty. This will be a maximum effort strike, we want to launch fifteen Hellcats from *Nabob*, to attack the airfield at Tromso at pre-dawn, they will then stay over the airfield to stop anything taking off. At sunrise, *Strikers* Hellcats will dive bomber *Tirpitz*, then attack the AA batteries, and also provide Combat Air Patrol (CAP) over the rest of the strike force. *Nabob* and *Strikers* Avengers will be the main strike, loaded with a mix of five-hundred pounds and one-thousand pounds armour piercing and delayed action bombs. *Strikers* Hellcats will provide top cover. OK so far, sir?"

Lee nodded.

"Sir, *Ruler*'s aircraft will launch thirty minutes later, to arrive over *Tirpitz* just as the main strike is leaving. If they are not needed, they can be tasked to attack 'target of opportunity' over northern Norway. Now we have *Fencer,* her Seafires will undertake CAP for the Carrier force, while her Barracuda's will launch thirty minutes before everybody else, being so slow, and conduct a torpedo strike, to arrive at the same time that *Strikers* Hellcat's commence their dive bomb attack."

Lee spoke, "Looks good, Miles, what are the drawbacks?"

A pained expression came across SPLOTS face, "'The Beast' is berthed here." Miles showed Lee one of the Norwegian Resistance photographs. "The Jerries have her berthed right underneath this rock cliff, so the attack will be difficult. They have multiple AA guns on either side of the fjord and on the top of that damn rock." Pointing to the rock cliff. "There is also an anti-torpedo net around her, one *Flak* ship berthed ahead and one astern of her. Smoke floats at various location around the fjord and last but not least, the Fighter airfield at Tromso is within ten minutes flying time away."

"I had wanted to launch a recon flight the day before, but I think that that might alert the Germans that we are in the area."

Lee, Davies and the pilots talked for the next two hours as they refined the plan of attack. Finally, they were happy with the plan and SPLOT left to make further arrangements. After his meeting, the remaining Cruiser and Destroyers skippers came aboard and mustered in the Wardroom. Lee outlined his orders and his requirements for the escorts. It was dark when Lee finally sat down and had something to eat. After which he went to his bunk, and slept fitfully, his mind unable to rest.

A knock on his cabin door awoke him. It was Timmins, who entered with a cup of tea! "Morning, sir, the weather is still fowl, we sail in one hour, so I have run you a bath, your seagoing uniform is washed and pressed and on the hanger, and in fifteen minutes I will have bacon and eggs ready!"

"Thank you, Timmins." Lee shook himself awake and arose from his bunk. Forty-five minutes later, he stood next to Matley on the bridge, wrapped up against the cold and rain, a towel around his neck to keep the rain out, and watched as his force started to leave the shelter of Loch Ewe.

"Chief Yeoman, make to Admiralty, copy to Admiral Home Fleet, the 30th ACS has weighed anchor." So, Commodore Alan Lee RN, and the 30th ACS went to war.

5 Norway

The daylight was just fading as the 30th ACS approached its flying-off position in the Norwegian Sea. The sea was still angry, and as Lee looked across at the carriers, they pitched and rolled badly. Matley stood next to him.

"I hope the weather improves overnight, otherwise the flyboys will struggle to take off," Matley spoke.

"Hmm," Lee answered, his mind busily going over his options.

The ships settled down to night cruising stations, all ships darkened down, and an eerie silence descended on *Bristol*. Lee could hear the sound of a cough and a snarling roar as an aircraft engine was being tested on the nearest carrier, the sound drifting in and out of range, as the mechanics fixed a problem ready for the action tomorrow. In his mind's eye, he could see the hangers of the carriers as the men went about their business preparing their charges for the dawn. Weapons loaded, fuel tanks topped up, oil and hydraulics checked, and windscreens polished, while in their cabins and ready rooms the aircrew tried to rest.

"Alf, I am going down to my cabin, call me if needed."

"Aye aye, sir," Matley replied, much as he enjoyed Lee's company it was nice to have his ship all to himself.

Sailing long at a depth of thirty metres, the hydrophone operator, leaned out of his small cubicle, "Captain! High-speed propellor noises to the north, many ships."

Kapitanleutnant Karl Lindemann, captain of U-991, a type VIIc submarine, strode across the control room. "What do you have, Heinz?" he asked. They were returning to their base at Trondheim, after a successful patrol in the Atlantic.

"Sir, it sounds like a small convoy, but it has many warships included, I can hear noises from four merchant ships, and about ten warships, very strange, not heard anything like this before." Heinz Kleber, was an experienced *Obermaat*, who had completed eight war missions, so he knew his job.

"OK, range and bearing, let's go and have a look," grunts Lindemann. To the control room, he speaks, "Periscope depth." The Chief Engineer releases his levers and watches the depth gauge as U-991 rises from the deep. A hiss of hydraulics as the search periscope rises out of its well, Lindemann makes a quick all-round sweep, to check all is safe. Satisfied he orders, "Surface the boat." The well-drilled boat crew go about their jobs efficiently, and the sub breaks water. Lindemann was first out of the hatch, binoculars to his eyes as he makes another rapid three-hundred-and-sixty-degree visual sweep around his boat, just to make sure there was nothing lurking about. Under his feet, he could hear the cough and rumble as the diesel motors came to life. Down the hatch he calls, "Lookouts to the bridge, course 010 north, full speed ahead on the diesels!". The submarine starts to roll as she heads north. Green seas sweep across the bridge, soaking everybody. Lindemann, in his heavy leather jacket, white Captain cap, jammed on his head, and with a towel around his neck, rests his Zeiss binoculars on the bridge screen, although he was out of torpedoes, it was only a short diversion from his route home, he needed to know what was out there. 'Four merchant ships and a lot of warships, that's unusual,' he thinks. Could it be an invasion force, a commando attack, or something else? Lifting the lid on his speaking tube, he calls the Radio Room. "Keep a track of our position, get it from the navigator, so we can send it in a flash message if we need to," he orders.

They continue north, night has fallen, and it is a dark night, the weather is awful, and the submarine continues to pitch and roll. At one o'clock, Lindemann was in the control room, looking at the chart table, when a lookout calls him urgently to the bridge, "Ships in sight." From his position atop the conning tower, he can just make out dim shapes emerging and disappearing in the night. Speaking to the officer of the watch, "Keep an eye on them, I am going below to look through the 'scope to see if I can get a better view." Moments later, the attack periscope hisses out of its holder above the lookout heads and starts its search.

H.M.S. *Nepal* is 'Tail end Charlie', her surface search radar scanning the sea around her. Her crew at defense stations, they are trying to get a little rest before the action tomorrow. The radar operator, Charlie 'Chalky' White, in his smokey, fug filled office is struggling to stay awake, he had been awake for about twenty hours, having spent the best part of his watch, fixing the rotating aerial above their heads, but a least the set was working again. Suddenly, he sat bolt upright in his chair, a blip had shown on his display! It was close about five miles away, how could he have missed it! "Radar…Bridge, contact astern range five miles," he called.

The navigator stuck his head through the blackout screen. "What you got, Chalkie?"

"I think it's a sub, sir, it's just popped up on the scope".

The orders flowed, "Very good, sound action stations enemy submarine, call the Captain, increase speed, message to the flagship!". This well-drilled ship's company went about their tasks.

Lindemann swore as he looks through the attack scope, 'Aircraft carriers, four of them, damn I have no 'fish' left, where are they going.' "Radio Room, send a message, four enemy aircraft carriers heading north, give our position and heading, have it coded and sent urgent." He made a visual sweep of the area around his sub. Little did he know that when he raised the telescope it was enough to be seen on *Nepal*'s radar screen, and now she was heading straight towards him at thirty knots. He looked horrified; a destroyer, with 'the bone in its teeth' coming straight towards him! "Clear the bridge, crash dive, did that message get out?" he shouted.

"Captain to the bridge, hands to action stations, submarine action," the Tannoy screamed, alarm rattlers sounded, seaboots pounded across the steel decks.

Dragged from an exhausted sleep, Captain Sam Bullock rushed onto the *Nepal*'s Bridge. "What have we got, pilot?"

The navigating officer replied, "Sir, surfaced sub, range four miles right on the bow sir, hands have been called to action stations."

"Very good."

"Radar...Bridge, sub-diving! Ship at action stations." No 1 shouted.

"Very good, ASDIC, have you got him?"

"Yes, sir, fine on the bow, down doppler, passing hundred feet" the ASDIC office replied.

"OK, quarter deck commence depth charge attack, set charges 'A' for Apple"

"Bunts, send a message to thirtieth ACS and the Admiralty, Attacking Submarine, and pass our position."

"Aye sir." The Black 'Attacking Submarine' Flag unfurls from the yard arm, *Nepal* commences her depth charge attack, and a full twelve charge pattern descended to the depths. Twelve huge brown-coloured water columns rose out of the angry sea. "Hard to port, slow to twenty knots, recommence the attack," Bullock ordered. If he could not sink the U-boat, then he knew he had to keep the sub down, it could not be allowed to send a signal. The lookout called, "Sir, *Van Galen* approaching to port."

'Good they could co-ordinate the attack better.' So, for the next two hours, *Nepal* and *Van Galen* took it in turns to pound U-991.

Below in U-991, the damage was accumulating, minor leaks had sprung, light bulbs exploded, gauges smashed, cables became detached, and the faint whiff of chlorine gas coming from the batteries.

"Radio room, did you get the message away?"

"Captain, we were transmitting when we dived so I don't know if it all got away," the radio room replied. The submarine shuddered badly, and the bow compartment opened up to the sea, the bulkhead hatch collapsed, and sub and her brave crew descended rapidly to the cold and dark seabed, nearly thousand feet below.

Onboard *Van Gelan*, the crew looked astern as a huge air bubble rose to the surface, and spewed forth broken wood, parts of the submarine, lifejackets and a huge amount of diesel oil began floating on the surface. Her Captain and crew were jumping about with happiness, it was their attack that had finished off the U-boat, this was the first submarine that this Dutch warship had sunk. Picking up evidence of the 'kill' in a bucket for later analysis by 'The Boffins'. It helped the pain of the Dutch crew, that they were doing something to help their families and friends back home in Holland, that were living under the Nazi jackboot. With *Nepal* cheering ship, they both turned and headed north after the carriers, they were along way behind.

At Trondheim in Norway, at the headquarters of the 13th Submarine Flotilla, the duty watch in the radio office were having a quiet night, very little radio traffic was coming their way. The Duty Operator, a *Maat*, stood up from his station and headed for the toilet, he needed to relieve himself urgently. As he walked away, his teleprinter started to chatter, it was in the four-letter cypher of the submarine 'Triton' code. After completing his 'business', he called at the galley and poured himself a black ersatz coffee, and headed back to his desk. Walking towards his desk he noticed the alert red light blinking, 'Hell, how long had that been flashing.' He looked around the room, but nobody looked like they had noticed! Pulling out his 'Enigma' machine he started to decode the message.

'From U-991, square AZ231, 4...' the message stopped. He tried to raise the submarine but got no response, he tried several times, again with no response. Then he called his supervisor over to discuss the message. The Radio Supervisor was a spotty-faced, twenty year old *Leutnant zur See*, an ardent Nazi, who everyone disliked.

"Sir, I have been unable to raise '991'. Should I put this out as a general alert to all stations?" the *Maat* asked.

The spotty-faced youth spoke, "There's no need for that, send it to the *Luftwaffe* desk, let them deal with it in the morning." And with that he strode out of the room, eager for his shift to be over, so he could return to the warmth of his Norwegian lover's bed. The *Maat* made a note in his log book, just in case!

Across the North Sea, in a ramshackle old house in Buckinghamshire, surrounded by Nissan huts, eager ears were listening.

It was 0330 when Lee arrived back on the bridge of *Bristol*. Around him he could sense the atmosphere, the ship was closed up at action stations, everybody was wearing anti-flash gear, 'Battle Bowlers' and lifejackets. Above his head, the Director Control Tower moved quietly on its roller bed as it searched the horizon. The scrape of an ammunition belt on the gun screen could just be heard, and the muted muttering of a ship's crew going about its business.

"Morning, sir," The Chief Yeoman called. An alert for everybody on the bridge, The Commodore is here! Matley came out from under the Navigation table 'black out' screen.

"Hello, sir, just double-checking everything," Matley spoke.

"It's OK, Alf, you don't need to explain to me," Lee spoke in a whisper and smiled. Across the sea, which had moderated a lot overnight, Lee could just make out the cough and roar of an aircraft engine starting up. The Barracudas were getting warmed up, they would be the first to go.

Lee said, "Chief Yeoman, as soon as it's light enough, signal *Nepal* and *Van Gelan*, well done for sinking that sub, and 'splice the mainbrace' make sure everybody sees it."

"Aye aye, sir."

Lee turned to Matley. "The Dutch and *Nepal* did well last night, it was awful weather for hunting a sub!" and in a lowered tone, "I received a message from the Admiralty, that that sub had spotted us." Louder, "Yeoman, ask *Fencer* to put out an extra anti-sub patrol this morning." The engine sounds from across the narrow stretch of water increased.

Alf Matley spoke, "They have started launching! And yes, sir, that would have given 'The Cloggies' a real boost." Lee smiled at the nickname for the Dutch warship.

The aircraft launch proper started thirty minutes later, as aircraft after aircraft clawed for height after leaving their mother ships. In the strengthening daylight, the Seafire CAP could be heard as it circled overhead, protecting the fleet, the torpedo carrying Barracudas well on their way to the enemy ship. For the next forty-five minutes, the air again was filled with the sound of aero engines, as the strike force roared off the carriers, formed up overhead, and headed towards Norway, wave hopping to avoid radar detection, at twenty miles out, then they would zoom climb up to attack altitude. A Hellcat and an Avenger both fired a red flare to announce they had a problem and were returning to their carrier. The rest of the strike force headed into the dark sky.

Onboard *Sperrbrecher 14*, the crew were being roused from their bunks, their empty stomachs grumbling, they made their way to their action stations, it was normal to go to action stations at daybreak; however, they knew that it was rare to see any action. Looking astern, Fritz, one of the 88mm gun loaders was surprised to see *Tirpitz* was still not roused.

"Typical, we do the work, they take the glory," he grumbled. He smiled at his friend Hans, the gun aimer, "Well, it's better than the Russian front," they both laughed. In the distance, they could just make out the sound of an air raid siren drifting on the breeze. Confused, they looked around waiting for an officer to give orders.

High overhead, SPLOT yelled into his radio, "Tally ho, we caught them asleep, commence the attack," switching radio channels, "Mother from Red 1,'Tremble'." The call sign to inform the carriers that they were attacking. He dived down to commence his dive-bombing attack on *Tirpitz*. He aimed for the bridge area, and released his weapon, pulling up he commenced to fire at the AA batteries that were sited on the overhanging cliff. His five-hundred-pound bomb glanced off the bridge wing and plunged alongside, where it erupted in a huge water spout. *Tirpitz* shuddered and moved sideways.

Approaching Tromso Airfield, *Nabob*'s Hellcats tore down the fjord at a low level, five aircraft in line abreast, in three waves. The far left-hand aircraft was so low, that its wing hit the mast of a Norwegian trawler and cartwheeled into the sea. They opened fire on three moored Bv-138 flying boats. Then onto the airfield. A line of BF 109 and BF 110 fighters were parked outside the hangers, these were attacked with great enthusiasm!

Above *Tirpitz,* the aircraft attacked with gusto, bomb after bomb pummeled the leviathan. Soon the smoke generators, sited around the fjord, started churning out its chemical smoke, the visibility quickly being reduced. The aircraft that had not released their weapons circled frantically as they searched for a break in the smoke. The two anti-aircraft *Sperrbrecher* were the only ships visible, so they bore the brunt of the attack. *Fencer*'s Barracudas lumbered up Kaa fjord, they were late, as they rounded the last bend, *Tirpitz* and her protection came into view. The smokescreen was deepening fast, so the squadron leader ordered his aircraft to launch blind into the smoke, hoping that at least one torpedo would strike. As they did so, they could hear and see the other strike aircraft buzzing around like angry bees trying to find their target. The air above *Tirpitz* was black with bursting shells, and coloured tracer bullets crisscrossed the sky, as all three ships put a box barrage above the Battleship. Here and there the odd aircraft was hit and limped away trailing smoke.

The Flak batteries on the cliff tops had a grandstand view of the Torpedo planes as they approached the fjord, and were able to pour fire down on the lumbering Barracudas. One of the Barracuda's torpedoes headed straight and true and hit the boiler room of Flak ship #14, the ship lurched to port and started to sink by the stern, the surviving crew leaping into freezing water. Two torpedoes ran amok and exploded on the beach opposite. One torpedo narrowly missed the anti-torpedo net and exploded on the stern of *Tirpitz*, just above the rudder, it entered the rudder control room, which caused local flooding. One torpedo also hit Flak ship #14 amidships. Unfortunately, the rest of the torpedoes, either missed or got entangled in the torpedo net. Eight Barracudas were shot down and crashed in and around the fjord, and the remaining aircraft, all suffering damage made their escape to the west. Six of *Strikers* Hellcats spotted the decimated Barracuda squadron and headed over to give them protection back to the carriers. *Nabob*'s Hellcats having shot up anything that could become a threat, headed to Kaa fjord to see if they could assist. As they approached the scene it was shrouded in fog, with anti-aircraft shells exploding above. Circling high above, Miles Davies looked out of his cockpit. He had spotted the torpedo strike on 'The Beast' and had seen the deep red glow where the five bombs had hit; however, he could not see the extent of the damage. He called up the Carriers and cancelled the follow-up strike, the fog would be around for some time so it would not be cleared in time for the scheduled strike. He called up on the radio network, "All aircraft, form up and return to base." The pilots, now with adrenalin coursing through their veins, were happy and excited, but that would soon wear off, as they headed back to the carriers. Miles warned them to keep a good lookout, having stirred up a hornet's nest, they would be under attack soon.

Across the fjord the two Norwegian Underground agents were watching from their hide, the radio operator was writing down the details of the attack, and the leader was calling out all the damage he could see. Later, after the attack was finished, they would radio a damage assessment to the S.O.E. headquarters.

Onboard *Sperrbrecher* 14, the gun crews were closed up, when to drone of aircraft engines could be heard. The gun director was speaking to the Talker on the aft 88mm gun, "Large formation of aircraft from the east, height four-thousand metres , bearing 092 degrees, commence!" The practiced crew went about their business with efficiency. The first shell was slammed into the breech and a moment later the familiar high-pitched crack enveloped the gun crew. They got into a rhythm, as shell after shell rose into the sky towards the attacking aircraft. The orders were soon changed, 'Box Barrage' over *Tirpitz* Commence! They did not see, or hear, the five-hundred-pound bomb that struck their gun mounting, Fritz's last memory was flying backwards over the ship's rail, and the cold embrace of the Kaa Fjord waters. Hit by two torpedoes, three five-hundred-pound bombs and nearly missed by another three bombs, the old converted freighter rolled on the port side and sank. The other Flak ship, *Sperrbrecher* 11, was pummeled by other attacking aircraft, but as she sank, she settled on an even keel, the water underneath was a lot shallower, this helped to save a lot of her crew. The two requisitioned trawlers that had been used as personnel ferries, one had disappeared, hit a bomb and disintegrated, and all that could be seen off boat number two was a large cloud of black smoke and sparks coming from her funnel as she heroically fled the scene!

Tirpitz had been badly damaged, the torpedo strike at the stern had smashed the steering compartment, so the rudder was jammed at 30 degrees to starboard, the concussion had twisted the two port propellor shafts, so they could not be rotated. One thousand-pound armoured piercing bomb had penetrated the deck next to 'Anton' turret and exploded, this caused the turret to leap up from the turret ring and land back at an angle, and the turret could not be moved. One five-hundred-pound high explosive bomb had penetrated the aircraft hangar and destroyed the two Arado 196 floatplanes, and started a huge fire amongst the stored aircraft fuel. The third bomb struck the port side on the forward fifteen-centimeter turret, abreast of the Bridge structure, shrapnel holed the bridge, injuring the Captain and a lot of the bridge crew, and the hull was perforated, and worse still, the cordite cases stored around the fifteen-centimetre gun housing, had ignited in a searing burst of flame, burning the gun crew, and penetrating down into the lobby, which leads to the muster point for a first aid party, wiping them out. Bombs four and five also penetrated the f'c'sle and erupted in the stoker and seaman's mess decks, also the paint locker, causing huge fires. The final bomb was a thousand-pound delayed action weapon, this penetrated the funnel casing, though the armoured deck and exploded in the forward engine's spaces, setting fire to a fuel tank, wrecking the engine room, it also penetrated the hull bottom, causing extensive flooding. The ship was now out of the war, she would need drydocking for the hull damage to be repaired and a heavy lift crane to lift out 'Anton' turret to be replaced, all these things were not available in Norway! Rescue launches, two E-Boats, and two coastal minesweepers were starting rescue operations. The air was heavy with the stench of chemical smoke, burnt wood, cordite fumes and the stink of heavy fuel oil.

30th Aircraft Carrier Squadron's aircraft arrived back at the fleet, and *Fencers* Seafires patrolled the air above the fleet. Whilst the Hellcats from *Ruler* were operating down range to provide protection for the returning aircraft.

In the Naval command bunker at Trondheim, a very angry senior officer was demanding answers, as to how and why, this attack had been allowed to happen.

Messages were sent out to the many airfields in northern Norway to seek out the enemy, while strike aircraft were being loaded with bombs and torpedoes, it was obviously the strike came from enemy aircraft carriers. The German airfields at, Banak, Trondheim, Bardufoss, and Bodo were a hive of activity as search aircraft were launched. The Gestapo descended on the radio room and radar offices, demanding to see all messages received that night. Soon all attention fell on the message received from U-991 and the desk log. Later, the sound of a single 9mm Luger bullet shattered the air around the base. A spotty-faced officer lay face down in the snow, and a Radio *Maat* secretly smiled.

6 Warmer Climes.

The carriers, turned and at best speed, headed South by West back towards Scapa Flow. Just below the carrier's horizon, four of *Rulers* Hellcats, intercepted and shot down two Fw 200 Condors, while the Seafires managed to catch and dispose of a BV138 flying boat. The RAF sent a PR Spitfire to take pictures later that day, and the Norwegian Underground sent an interim message regarding the damage to *Tirpitz*. Unfortunately, they never got to send a follow-up message, they had been betrayed, and their first transmission was intercepted by the German Listening Service, which had pinpointed their position overlooking the fjord. A detachment of German Alpine troops, trapped and captured them in their cave. They were taken to the local Command post for interrogation. The men's families were spirited away by friendly Resistance members, through the snow and ice to neutral Sweden, where they survived, and could mourn the loss of their loved ones. Six surviving crew members from three Barracuda aircraft were also captured, and they fared slightly better. After having been interrogated, they were dispatched South, to a German POW camp in Poland. The cost for the 30th ACS was eight Barracudas, three Hellcats, and three Avengers, all the crews being lost or captured, and also four Seafires that had deck landing accidents on

Fencer. Meanwhile the *Luftwaffe*, desperately searched the Norwegian Sea for the carrier force, but the navy fighters kept the enemy away.

Lee was elated and despondent, the loss of his aircrew was taken very hard. Although in material terms, the loss of a few aircraft against the crippling of a Battleship was a good exchange, but he still mourned the loss of his brave aircraft crews. Congratulations flooded into *Bristol*'s Radio Room, it seemed everybody was taking an interest in what had happened. ABC, had sent the Home Fleet out to meet and escort the 30th ACS home. Lee had instructed *Van Gelan, Nepal*, and the carriers to lead the force into the Flow, with the cruisers and destroyers following. All the ships at anchor in the Flow, presented crews and cheered ship as they proceeded through the dark waters. From *Iron Duke*, flew the message from Admiral Cunningham, 'Manoeuvre well executed, Commodore 30th ACS report onboard'. In the interim period the RAF had managed to get some up-to-date photo's that showed *Tirpitz*, down by the stern and with a list to starboard, surrounded by various rescue craft, that were trying to assist in her salvage. Months later the famous RAF 617 Dambuster Squadron would attack the Battleship with massive twenty-two-thousand-pound bombs that would sink her. For now, the Royal Navy basked in the glory.

While his ships started being refueled and resupplied, Lee was onboard *Iron Duke* giving the Admiral, Home Fleet, a detailed report on the operation. He was given his new orders. With the long-awaited assault on the French South Coast due soon, and with the threat from *Tirpitz* eliminated for now, they were to proceed to the Mediterranean, after the successful landings in Sicily and Italy, the Allied armies were fighting their way slowly north. Lee's orders were to attack and sink any shipping between Italy and the Yugoslav coast. Also, to disrupt as much air and sea traffic he could.

Later, Lee was resting in his bunk, his eyes closed, his imagination trying to block out the images of dying ships and their crews, friends now gone, this damn war. His cabin was very quiet, only the faint sounds of Timmins working in the pantry penetrated the bulkhead. The ship, *his ship Preston*, was gone. Now he rested, and tried to relax. Around him the ship gently moved with the tide; the vents above his bunk gave a gentle hum as they distributed air around him. A hydraulic pump started up, as above his head, 'Y' turret was tested. Occasionally, the sounds of the crew drifted in through the open scuttle. For many centuries sailors had heard these sounds around them, and found comfort. Ships were never completely silent; ships were living breathing beings. Lee drifted off into a listless sleep.

They sailed the following morning. Out through the Hoxa Gate, the Boom Defense Vessel, giving a friendly toot on her whistle as they passed. Yet again, the Pentland Firth showed its anger, as Lee watched his Carriers pitch and roll into the dangerous seas. As they entered the waterway known as 'The Minches', the sun came out and the wind died away. As they proceeded south, some of the crew came on the upper deck to catch some sun and to relax. Suddenly, from the port wing of the bridge, a voice rang out, in a broad Western Isles accent, "There's ma hoos, There's ma hoos!"

"Silence!" shouted the Cox'n.

"But, sir, that's ma hoos." The bridge watch and all those that were in earshot fell about laughing, Matley turned to Lee a huge smile on his face. The young HO rating had not seen his home for the past twelve months and had got over excited. After that, every time *Bristol* came within sight of land the shout would go up, "There's ma hoos!" Until after a few weeks everybody got fed up with it.

Down through the Irish sea, the waters were calm and the sun gave away some of its precious warmth. As they passed Liverpool, he sent his Destroyers in for fuel. The carriers went about the business of receiving replacement aircraft from *HMS Redcap*, the Royal Naval Air Station in leafy Cheshire, to replace the aircraft lost in the *Tirpitz* raid. Also four Walrus aircraft were added to his force, one for each Carrier, these were to be used for air-sea rescue for his downed crews. This was part of his recommendations to the Admiralty following the attack, he also asked for *Fencer*'s aircraft compliment to be exchanged for Hellcats and Avengers. This request met with a stoney silence! As they approached the Bristol Channel, *Nabob* started to have trouble with her propellor shaft. Lee ordered her into Pembroke Dock, for inspection and repairs, two of his destroyers were ordered to escort her. He slowed his force down to give time for *Nabob* to reach Pembroke and return. Unfortunately, this could not be done quickly and she would have to wait for the

Floating Dry Dock to become available. He therefore, with the rest of his force, increased speed and headed for Plymouth. As his ships passed the Lizard, all the serviceable aircraft were flown off to *HMS Seahawk*, near Helston in Cornwall, so the aircrew could start their leave a little earlier.

The boom of the Plymouth Breakwater opened up to allow his force to enter the great natural harbour. The air was heavy with the smell of burning wood and crushed brickwork, a legacy of yet another German Air raid on the docks and town. The destroyers headed for the dockyard for some needed repairs and additions, while the carriers and cruisers found anchorages inside the crowded harbour. The crews could not believe the amount of anchored shipping. It was all so obvious that the much-vaunted 'Second Front' was not far away. There was a steady stream of liberty boats and tenders heading for the Royal Dockyard, taking eager matelots ashore for embarkation leave, four days for each watch, and Lee left *Bristol* for a meeting with the Admiral in charge of Plymouth, then headed home to stay with his wife and children for five days of peace and quiet.

All too soon his leave was over and a shiny staff car with Natalie again, allocated as his Wren Driver, sat outside his home as he said goodbye to his family. Local friends and neighbours also gathered around to see him off. His children were amazed to see a women driver and a shiny car! They loved it. They soon arrived at the Dockyard entrance, where they had their identities checked. Then at the steps at No 4 dock where a smart launch was waiting to take him back to his flagship, little did he know it, but it would be a long time before he set foot ashore in Plymouth again.

Three days later, they sailed. Following the Local Escort and Minesweeping forces out into the English Channel, about twenty miles south their escort wished them good luck and turned for home. The 30th ACS headed towards The Lizard to start re-embarking their aircraft. *Nabob* was still being repaired so she would rejoin later. All went well with the landing of the aircraft, apart from *Fencer*, where two of her elegant Seafires, managed to crash on landing! Fortunately, the pilots were uninjured. The carriers soon got back into the routine, launching anti-submarine patrols and a CAP of fighters above the force. They headed south, unusually, the Bay of Biscay was kind to them, the winds were light, the visibility was excellent, and the sun was warm! All the ships Captains have been instructed, by Lee, to enforce training schedules, they were again going into harm's way, and he wanted them ready. *Bristol*, trembled as the alarm rattlers went off, man overboard, launch seaboat, fires down below, flooding in the lower spaces, anything that Matley and his No 1 could think about. *Stinger* was instructed to tow *Striker*, an evulsion which would test their metal! Watched closely and cheered on by the watching ships company, all went well, much to Lee's relief.

Just as *Striker* cast off the tow line, the alarm rattlers sounded; two aircraft were heading towards them from Ushant. The airborne CAP raced off to intercept, while two more Hellcats were made ready just in case they were needed. Lee smiled; he liked what he saw. The radio repeater on the bridge of *Bristol*, sparked into life "Foxtrot (*Fencer*) from Red 1, two, repeat two, F.W. 200 Condors, am engaging". In the far distance, just visible, the shape of two larger aircraft and three smaller ones could be seen dancing around the sky. A few moments later one of the Condors was seen to catch fire and crash into the sea, while the other one retired as fast as he could with one of his port engines on fire, chased by two Seafires. The radio repeater crackled into life again, "Red 1 break of chase and return to mother, over"

"Red 1 understood, returning, I don't think that this 'Jerry' will be going much further." *Striker* launched four Hellcats to replace the returning CAP. Lee watched as the Seafires landed back onboard *Fencer*. The first two landed ok, but the third one, appeared to pitch forward on landing, and its airscrew 'pecked' the wooden flight deck. This was enough to destroy the wonderfully engineered Rolls Royce Merlin engine. 'Damn,' thought Lee. 'Another one lost!'

Little did they know, the pilot of the Condor, *LT. Felix Gruber*, managed to nurse his badly damaged aircraft back to its base near Brest in France. His radio operator and his tail gunner were dead, and the aircraft was leaking hydraulic fluid, one engine was stopped, and the radio was destroyed. His limping aircraft slowly made its way back to his base, where it crash landed, and the remaining crew managed to escape further injury. But he had got his important message back, three Enemy Aircraft Carrier and other ships heading south across The Bay, speed of twelve knots. This was message that the *Fliegerfuhrer Atlantik* had been waiting for! He could launch another of German's new secret weapons. A little over two hours later, 8 Do 217K-2 from KG-200, each loaded with a single Hs 293 'Fritz-X' guided bomb. This was a standard thousand-kilogram bomb, with a crucifix tailplane, that could be guided by remote control, so in theory, the weapon could be aimed with greater accuracy. They took off and headed towards the reported location of 30th ACS. Escorted by six Ju 88 'Heavy Fighters' and twelve Me 410 '*Destroyers*'.

Sub Lt Bob Jones and his crew had taken off from *Ruler*, and were flying past the Île-Molène, in the Bay of Biscay, about twenty miles offshore, searching for any submarines heading for the U-Boat pens in Brest. Cruising at twenty-thousand feet they spotted a large formation of German aircraft taking off from three airfields on the Brest Peninsula, they formed up and headed off to the west. Jones knew immediately that they were heading for the carriers.

"Jack, get on the blower tell the 'Old Man', large formation of bombers heading their way, quick as you can, send it plain language."

"Aye aye, skipper."

Out of voice message range, the Radio Operator began busily tapping away on his morse key. It was half an hour before sunset when the message hit the Radio Receivers of *Bristol* and *Ruler*. Lee ordered his carriers to launch fighters, and as his carriers turned into the wind to launch, the first wave of German aircraft arrived. It was a mad scramble as crews were climbed into aircraft, aircraft in the wrong place and being re-spotted on the flight decks. They had been caught unprepared. The four airborne Hellcats headed East to form a blocking force and give the other fighters time to get in the air. The Me 410s were leading the formation, so naturally the Hellcats turned to attack these first. This was, however, the first time they had encountered these new German Heavy Fighters, they were fast and agile, and had remote control waist guns. Selecting a beam attack, the first two Hellcats flew straight into their killing zones. The two nineteen-year-old Royal Navy pilots never knew what killed them. The two remaining Hellcat pilots watched in horror as their friends died. They changed their tactics from a beam attack to an astern attack, but this also made them vulnerable to the heavy front guns of the trailing Me 410s. *Fencer* had managed to get three Seafires airborne, and they also joined in the melee. Lee stood on the bridge watching the aerial battle; he had noticed the last group of bombers had stayed at about twelve-thousand feet and were circling around to the east. Having endured many bombing attacks over the past few years it was obvious to him they would be making a high-level bombing run, while the few Ju88s he could see, would commence a dive-bombing attack. He was distracted, watching, as *Striker* and *Ruler*, had managed to get eight more fighters airborne. The leading elements had just got into gun range, so the ships had commenced to fire.

Onboard the leading Dornier 217, Gruppenkommandeur of 1/KG200 Hptm. Karl Roch, circled the carriers, and his missile aimer Joachim Liter was searching for a suitable target.

"*Hptm*. We need to be nearer, we are just out of range."

"Understood." Roch looked down; the 'Tommies' were now launching fighters, he calculated he only had a few minutes left before they had to run. "Quick, Joachim, any ship will do." Lying prone in the front of the Dornier, the aimer had his right arm out, and was caressing the 'joy stick' controller for the missile.

'This was not like in training,' he thought. 'They weren't shooting then.'

"Steady, steady, missile away." The aircraft pitched upwards, as the weight of the bomb left the aircraft. For the weapon to work properly the launch aircraft had to fly straight and level for fifteen seconds, while the aimer guided the missile. Liter watched intently as he guided the missile; its track was easy to spot, as attached to the missiles tail fins was a flare and smoke canisters, which left a bright smoky trail, this allowed him to make minute changes to the trajectory of the weapon. He had aimed it at a cruiser that was closest to him, he kept his aim steady, as it guided straight and true, into the aft engine room of *Black Prince*.

Onboard *Black Prince*, three-hundred-and-twenty kilograms of amatol explosives in an armoured bomb casing hit just aft of the rear funnel, smashed through the paper-thin deck plates, continuing down, it passed through a workshop space, entered the engine room, and struck the starboard engine casing. There it exploded, destroying the engine room, killing all in there and rupturing the fuel tanks and bilge keel, opening the compartment to the sea. *Black Prince* was doomed, she broke in half and with both the bow and stern pointing at the sky and she lingered for a moment and then plunged to the bottom. Of the seven following missiles, one hit *Bristol* abreast "B" gun, but failed to explode. One hit *Fencer* on the aircraft lift, but again failed to explode, but did damage the lift. The final strike was on *Swift*, which disappeared in a blinding explosion, and was lost with all hands.

Lee was aghast, how could this have happened so quickly. As more fighters launched from the carriers and went roaring after the retreating Germans seeking revenge, his destroyers commenced rescue operations. The victorious Germans were heading home, engine throttles against the fire wall, desperately trying to avoid the avenging navy Fighters. But the Hellcats and Seafires did have some satisfaction, four of the Dorniers, all eight of the Ju 88 and two 410s were shot down. Because *Fencer*'s flight deck was damaged, her airborne aircraft had to land back on the other two carriers. The only good thing to come out of this tragedy was the two bombs that failed to explode were salvaged, therefore revealing their secrets. Lee decided that *Fencer* should return to Plymouth for repair, escorted by *Stinger* and *Nepal*, with *Napier* and *Stord* still missing with *Nabob*, he would carry on to Gibraltar with his sadly depleted force. They watched as *Fencer* and escorts took their leave. He had learnt a very valuable lesson, he must be ready in future, he would not be caught out again. Also, yet again, the Germans had developed a new and formidable weapon system that the Allied forces knew nothing about. It was a chaste and down hearted force that headed south and west, towards Gibraltar. As they passed Algeciras, inquisitive eyes watched as the force approached. A signal crackled across the ether towards a huge signal tower in southern Germany. 'Two aircraft carriers and three cruisers just arrived in Gibraltar'.

Entering Gibraltar Harbour, Lee was struck by the amount of shipping that was anchored around the bay, and the various warships berthed in the harbour its self. A large group of senior officers were awaiting *Bristol*'s arrival at her berth by the Signal Tower. As soon as the gangway was ashore, they trouped onboard. Much later, the inquisition left the ship, armed with the evidence of the missile and reams of paperwork and official statements. Lee had an uneasy feeling about this. As he retired to his cabin, Timmins was waiting with a hot cup of Kye laced with rum, just what was needed. The following morning, all dressed in his best white uniform and with Matley by his side, Lee was driven to Admiralty House to meet with Admiral Henry Harwood, victor of the River Plate battle. They were ushered into a conference room, where a moment later, the Admiral and his staff came in.

In a brusque tone, "Sit down, Commodore. With your Carrier group reduced by half, we may have to re-plan your campaign." The tone made it quite clear that H.H. held him personally responsible for the losses. "Not to leave this room," he continued in a stern voice, "The invasion of France will commence. In two weeks, there will be a simultaneous landing in Southern France, we want your group to sail into the Adriatic, and harass shipping and airfields in that area, we must draw off some of the strength of the Luftwaffe, to leave southern France less well defended. As you are short of escorts, there will be two Hunt class destroyers joining your command, you will sail in the morning, I want you out there causing mayhem, and drawing as much attention to yourselves as possible, we must draw the German attention away from southern France, I have just received a signal from 'their Lordships' *Nabob* is repaired and on her way to rejoin you, are you ready to sail?"

Lee said, "Yes, sir, we are ready, just need the two Didos to finish fuelling."

With a stern look, the Admiral got up and left, his Chief of Staff remained to continue briefing Lee.

'Well, that went well,' thought Lee.

Later, Lee was back onboard and was having a troubled sleep, so many things to remember and to plan for. Like a drill piercing his skull, the alarm rattles screamed and the Tannoy announced, "Action Stations, close all watertight doors, away seaboat and whaler, Marine's muster on the quarterdeck fully armed." Lee dressed hurriedly. What was going on, they were tied up in one of His Majesties most guarded harbour's. Timmins rushed in with Lee's seagoing coat and life jacket.

"Sir, a picket boat has spotted and attacked an unknown craft just at the South entrance. Captain Matley has requested you to come to the bridge."

"Very good." Lee could hear the noise abating outside his cabin door as the crew manned their action stations, just as he stepped onto the quarter-deck, he heard three small explosions, and the harbour was lit up, as searchlights swept the harbour surface, over by the dockyard wall, an Oerlikon was firing bursts out to sea at something. Two motor launches and a gunboat went snarling out of the harbour to find the enemy. The duty destroyer was leaving the destroyer trots and was also exiting the North Entrance. Picking up his 'Tin Hat' he entered the bridge.

A voice rang out, "Commodore on the Bridge."

"Hello, Alf, what's going on?" he asked.

"Hello, sir, sorry to rouse you." Matley's face suddenly lights up! A loud explosion was heard and felt. Looking towards the detached mole, the old Battleship *Vengeance*, and the even older fleet oiler *Tidereach*, which was alongside, were leaning into each other as a growing pool of burning oil started to surround the two ships. Matley leaned over the bridge wing and shouted, "Seaboat and whaler make for that fire, and start rescuing survivors, marines, line the main deck and be prepared to shoot on my command at anything in the water. No 1, get the steam launch in the water!"

Moments later CPO Signals calls out, "Sir, from the Port Admiral, suspect enemy mini-subs in harbour, get your ship's diver ready to inspect hulls!"

Later, another voice shouts out, "Messenger coming aboard, sir."

"Very well, now we might find out what's going on.".

The young Flag Leutnant, arrived breathless on *Bristol*'s Bridge. "Sir, we have recovered the crew of an Italian Human Torpedo, they are being interrogated now at the Destroyer pens, we have ordered harbour craft to drop hand grenades to deter any more." As he spoke, the crump of exploding hand grenades could be heard in the distance. "Sir can you have your ship's hulls inspected for any explosives and when you are clear please leave the harbour as soon as possible."

Lee spoke, "Thank you, lieutenant, we have three divers ready to enter the water, as soon as the explosions stop, I have ordered the Carriers to check also."

"Where did these Manned Torpedoes come from?" The Flag Lieutenant spoke with anger in his voice.

"We are pretty certain that they come from Algeciras, the Italians have a merchant ship the *S.S. Oiterra* interned there, we are ninety per cent positive that she has been converted to handle these manned torpedoes, and crewed by the Italian Navy's, elite, Decima Flottiglia MAS, we have made representations to the Spanish but they won't investigate, but don't worry we will get our own back soon," he stated with a twinkle in his eye!

7 Adriatic

With the hulls checked and cleared for any explosives, they sailed at 0600, just as the first rays of the sun rose over the eastern horizon, they were well clear of Gibraltar when the sun finally came up. The German spy in Algeciras, pleased with the result of the evening's clandestine attack, had got drunk and overslept, so missed the sailing of the 30th ACS. They headed East at a steady twelve knots, determined not to be caught out again, he had a strong CAP over the carriers, and his Avengers were ranging far and wide. There was a steady stream of shipping heading along the north coast of Africa, shepherd by escort destroyers, Frigates and the ubiquitous minesweepers, as supplies were passed by sea, to the Allied forces based now in North Africa. Mercifully the sky remained clear of Axis air forces, what a difference from the last time he was here. As they exited the Alboran Sea and came abreast Oran, *Fernie*, one of his attached Hunt class escort destroyers, detected a submarine contact on the starboard bow. In a flurry of spray, she turned to attack, also on that side, *Silverton*, went to assist. Lee ordered a sharp turn away for the rest of his ships. He watched as these two Hunts stalked their prey. It was clear that these two had worked together for some time, both veterans of the hard-fought battles in the sea lanes of the

English Channel. One of *Strikers* Avengers, circled overhead, ready to help if needed. *Fernie* slowed down, and as they watched a cloud of brown cordite smoke arose from her f'c'sle, the sound of dull explosions reaching *Bristol* a moment later. About two-hundred yards ahead of *Fernie*, a circle of splashes appeared as twenty-four mortar rounds fell into the depths. This was the first time Lee had seen the new secret anti-submarine weapon, called 'Hedgehog', in action. Thirty seconds later there was a dull thud, felt, rather than heard, underfoot. A column of dirty water rose from the surface of the sea. *U-456* had met her fate. Diesel fuel, splintered wood and other debris floated to the surface. *Fernie* slowed down to collect proof of her kill.

"Bunt's signal *Fernie* and *Silverton* 'well done, splice the main brace'," Lee ordered. "Captain Matley, resume course please," Onwards they moved at a stately twelve knots, now entering the Sicilian Narrows. 'How strange,' thought Lee. The last time he sailed through here, the sky was full of Axis aircraft, all trying to do him harm. Now it was a pleasant voyage in the warm sun! Over to the starboard side, they could see the grounded and abandoned wreck of *HMS Havock*, burnt out and destroyed after she ran aground months ago; now she sat there as a guide to other ships, and a visual warning to keep clear.

He ordered his destroyers and cruisers in groups to enter the Grand Harbour in Malta for refuelling. Once refuelled, he left harbour and headed north for the Adriatic. He instructed his carriers to launch recon. flights along the Italian and Dalmatian coast, looking for suitable targets.

As they entered the Ionian Sea, a small convoy of Coasters and *Karavoskaro*s was spotted hugging the Ionian islands, heading towards Kefalonia and escorted by two *Vp* boats. Within ninety minutes, a strike force of eight Hellcats and eight Avengers was launched by *Striker*. A short time later, *Ruler*'s search planes had found a medium size freighter and a small corvette heading north up the Italian coast, towards Taranto. They also launched a strike force to intercept these enemy ships.

Strikers' aircraft made short work of their target. The five small merchant ships and one of the *Vp* boats were left sinking or ablaze, the remaining *Vp* boat was left to carry out rescue operations. In the late afternoon, *Ruler*'s aircraft arrived overhead of the lone Coaster and her escort, and ran into an Italian Fighter escort, Four Macchi C202 *Folgore* fighters, high above the slow-moving merchant ship. These were fast nimble fighters, powered by the excellent Daimler Benz DB 601A engines from the Me 109 Fighter. The Hellcats tore into the *Regia Aeronautica* fighters, while the Avengers attacked the Merchant ship. In a swirling aerial dogfight that lasted ten minutes, two C202 were shot down and the remaining two had to break off and head back home for fuel, but one Hellcat was missing and one with battle damage, that had turned back towards *Ruler*.

The Avengers had damaged the ship, and it had been forced to head towards the beach and ran aground to save it from sinking, and the Italian Corvette was also left in a sinking state. *Ruler* launched her Walrus Flying boat, which headed towards the damaged fighter, its intention to escort the Hellcat back to the carrier.

Onboard *Bristol,* Lee was reading the after-action reports from the aircraft, an excellent day in their new hunting grounds. A voice broke his chain of thought. "*Nabob* in sight sir, twenty miles due south!"

"Thank you, bunts, that's good news, she's made good time." With the aircraft recovered, and *Nabob* back in company, they headed further north into the Adriatic. Lee had instructed his SPLOT to come up with a strike plan for an attack on the port of Taranto. If the Admiralty wanted Lee's forces to stir up the enemy, then this would have the desired effect. In 1940, the Eastern Mediterranean Fleet had struck at Taranto, using a handful of old, slow, Swordfish bi-plane torpedo bombers, from the carrier *Illustrious* in a decisive move, which sank or crippled the Italian battle fleet. Sinking or badly damaging all their Battleships bar one. Although he knew from intelligence reports, that the major units of the Italian fleet were berthed further north, there were sufficient warships still in the harbour to warrant this attack.

The following day found the carrier strike force closing on Taranto. The plan was very simple, two Walrus aircraft would arrive first and circle the harbour, dropping flares for the attacking aircraft. Thirty Hellcat fighter bombers, and thirty-five Avengers, loaded with torpedoes and bombs would strike at one o'clock in the morning, hopefully catching the Italians asleep. The remaining Hellcats would be held as a CAP for the carriers. And the final Walrus, along with the two-flare dropping Walrus would be used for Aircrew rescue.

At 0030, the warm night air was disturbed by the low rumble of two Pegasus sleeve valve engines on two Walrus aircraft coughed into life. The carriers turned into the wind and these relics from a past life lurched into the air. The noise levels increased dramatically as the strike force snarled into life, roared down three flight decks and headed due north. Coordination between the Walrus and the strike leader was perfect, as the Hellcats approached from north and south, the flares dropped by the Walrus burst over the harbour, bathing everything in a deathly glow. The fighters swooped down strafing and bombing any target of opportunity. For ten minutes the fighters created havoc. Then the Avengers, having split into two forces and heading in from east and west, the aircraft from the east struck at the warships in the inner harbour *Mar Piccolo.* The ones from the west attacked shipping in the *Mar Grande*, the outer harbour. Above droned the Walrus keeping the sky lit up, and staying invisible above the light of the flares.

Above the *Mar Piccolo, Nabob*'s Avengers #5 and #8, flying at low level, and wingtip to wingtip, made a perfect bombing run on the Italian Destroyer pens. A total of eight armoured piercing and delayed action seven-hundred-and-fifty-pound bombs, decimating the 6th Destroyer Squadriglie. The *Granatiere* and *Bersagliere*, sank at their moorings and *Fuciliere* and *Pontiere*, so badly damaged they would take no further action in the war. Then the Avengers from *Striker* and *Ruler* hit shipping in the *Mar*

Grande. Torpedoes ripped into the Heavy Cruiser *Gorizia* blowing off her bows, the light cruiser *Bari* sank at her moorings. The fleet oiler *Barrossia* was hit by a torpedo and she sank by the stern. And two small coastal freighters were also badly damaged. Having truly woken up the Italian anti-aircraft defences, the British aircraft turned south for home, but unfortunately, two Avengers and two Hellcats were lost.

The carriers turned into the wind and took back onboard their aircraft. The losses had been extremely light for the damage inflicted. Lee knew that the Italians and Germans would be looking for revenge come daybreak. All the Hellcats were refuelled and rearmed and their pilots getting a few moments of sleep. Just before dawn broke, a lone Italian Air Force SM79 ('Hunchback') spotted the carriers as they headed south, the radio operator tapping out his urgent message, 'Enemy found'. This set into motion, a series of messages in the Italian air force headquarters.

At an Italian airfield just south of Rome, Major Hans Muller was awoken by his servant, it was 0530 in the morning.

"Sorry to wake you, Herr Major. An urgent message from Headquarters."

Hans sat at the edge of his cot, he was bone weary. *What does 'Smiling Albert' (General Kesselring, the General commanding, German Forces Italy.) want now!* he thought. Pulling on his pants and shirt, and grabbing the offered pot of ersatz coffee, he wearily headed over the

Squadron Ops Office. He arrived just as the sun was coming up, the air still warm and humid. He glanced around the airfield. The 'Black Gang' were working on a couple of battered-looking *Jabo* FW 190s, in the distance he could just make out a Me-410 having an engine run-up. It had been moved overnight and parked amongst some Italian aircraft wrecked from previous attacks on the airfield, it was hoped that the visiting Allied airmen would fail to spot it.

"Herr Major, the General" a communications clerk held out a telephone for Muller.

He spoke, "Muller here, sir."

"Ah, Hans, that took you long enough!" the deep booming voice of Kesselring sounded in his ear. "Last night, the 'Tommies' made a strike on Taranto, they caused a lot of damage, the strike came from a group of aircraft carriers in the Adriatic, they are now heading south, a 'Hunchback' is tailing them as we speak. I want a maximum strike, every airplane you have, *Goering* wants a carrier sunk, so he can boast about it to The Austrian Corporal!"

Muller slowly shook his head. "Understood General, but I have only a handful of aircraft here, and they are in a poor state, all my best aircraft and pilots have been sent south to attack the Sicilian Invasion forces!"

"Yes, yes, I know, we will be sending more machines from airfields in the north, they will attack as they arrive, for now, I want my best Flight leader out there." And with that 'Smiling Albert' put the phone down. A coding machine chattered into life, giving the position, speed, bearing and composition of the Tommies carriers.

"Herr Oberst," he called to the office next door. "Get every pilot up and assembled in here, and arm every aircraft with whatever weapons we have." He looked at the floor, this was going to be a bad day. One hour later, an assortment of war-weary, patched-up wrecks of the once mighty *Luftwaffe*, staggered into the air and headed South East. Muller looked down at his command, three Fw 190s, Fighter Bombers (*Jabo*), six Stukas, four He177s and a He 111, all limping along at the Stuka's top speed of one-hundred-and-eighty kilometers per hour. Once airborne, he always reminded himself of how he got here. Not now, he just wanted to return and land safely, his days of 'daring do' against the Tommies were over, he just wanted to survive the war. As they crossed the coast, still struggling for height, a lone Avenger spotted them. To the Avenger crew, it was clear where they were heading, the carriers!

'Yoke #4' transmitted in the clear, "Air Raid, multiple targets heading South East." Onboard the carriers, the orders went out to launch all fighters, and the airborne CAP was ordered further 'up threat'. The three carriers turned into the wind, and Hellcats began leaving the decks and clawing for height.

Muller arranged the miscellaneous aircraft into some sort of mutual supporting formation, with his FW190s above and behind, positioned to swoop down on any attackers. As they droned on, he received a message from HQ, that more Do 217 and He 111 aircraft were en route to assist, however, his three Fws were the only fighters.

Moments later he could just make out 6 airborne dots on the horizon. He had been spotted. As the enemy fighters got closer, they looked different from the ones he had seen in the past, these were bigger, faster and appeared more manoeuvrable. The Hellcat was new to the Mediterranean war, and would soon show its mettle. Muller ordered his wingmen to jettison their bombs and climb, and set course to intercept the enemy fighters. The Hellcats split into pairs and aimed straight at the FWs. Leaving the bombers alone, they were allowed to carry on towards the carriers. Muller tangled with a Hellcat, the FW was a formidable opponent, but it could not keep up with the new 'fighter', round and round they danced, climbing, diving, but he could not get into a firing solution, but he had made the fateful error he had forgotten about the enemy wingman! .50 calibre bullets tore into his engine, oil spread all over his windscreen, obstructing his view, he cranked back his canopy, the noise and the smell of oil and exhaust gases assaulted him. His aircraft shuddered again and his rudder bar jerked to the left, he pushed it, useless, time to get out. He released his seat straps, checked his parachute was attached, stood up, and threw himself out of the cockpit. The parachute opened with a snap, and then a jerk as it deployed, he thanked the stars for its operation! He gently floated down, the space around him was strangely vacant, and the air battle had moved on. The sea rushed up to meet him, and he awoke floating on his back, his life raft was inflated and floating next to him, and somehow, he had managed to release his parachute. He struggled for what seemed like an age, to get into his raft, exhausted he lay back, and took stock of his situation.

The Hellcats fell on the FWs, two were shot down straight away, and the third was clearly more experienced and succeeded in staying airborne until he crossed the sights of a Hellcat, six .50 calibre guns made short work of him. Further fighter aircraft launched from the carriers and climbed to attack the undefended bombers, soon, all bar one was shot down in flames. The lone He 177 on fire, turned and headed for home, having dumped its bombs in the sea. The bombers deployed from Northern Italy fared no better. Of twenty-three Do 217, and thirty HE 111, none bombed the carriers, twenty aircraft were destroyed and the remainder turned back and landed on any Italian airfield they could reach, all with battle damage or technical faults.

As the reports flowed into *Bristol*'s bridge, Lee read each one, after all the hard years and countless ships lost to the dreaded Luftwaffe, it was nice to have some revenge. Thirty-six enemy planes were shot down for the loss of four Hellcats and an Avenger bomber! He was ecstatic, this was part reward for the loss of *Preston*! He ordered the carriers to launch SAR aircraft to find his missing pilots. They located the Avenger crew and two of the Hellcat pilots, and also a Luftwaffe Major! When the rescue operation was concluded he ordered his ships south, back to Malta to refuel and rearm.

8 Surprise attack

The ships were berthed in Malta's Grand Harbour. A flurry of activity as fuel barges, water carriers, ammunition lighters, all swarmed around his ships. Lee stood on *Bristol*'s Quarterdeck looking around him, he recalled the screaming Stukas, the bark of Anti-Aircraft guns, and the crump of exploding bombs. The Harbour was still littered with multiple wrecks, but these were being rapidly disposed of. Following his visit to the Admiral, he had ordered his barge to take him to the dockyard, he wanted to look at the wreck of a past 'chummy' ship *Jersey*, he was saddened to see a tangled twisted wreck that no longer looked like a ship, and would never again sail. (She would be cut into two parts, towed out of the dock, and scuttled outside the breakwater). He said a silent prayer and ordered the barge back to *Bristol*.

Later in his cabin, he was going through the endless list, orders, and requests, that seemed to take up most of his life these days, there was a knock at his door. The Marine sentry spoke, "Captain Matley. sir.". A relaxed-looking Matley stepped over the coaming and closed the door.

"Hello, sir."
"Hi, Alf, come and take the weight off your feet, gin?"
Matley smiled and nodded. "Thank you, sir."

"Timmins, two pink gins please."

"Yes, sir, coming up."

"OK, Alf, what's up," Lee spoke.

"Just received a signal, *Fencer* is due to arrive at 1000 hours, along with her escorts, they want us to sail as soon as practical, the invasion of Southern France is due in a few days and they want us back in the Adriatic, causing trouble."

"Thanks, Alf, how long will it take *Fencer* and her escorts to refuel?"

"My guess, about six to eight hours."

"OK, then tell *Fencer* and her escorts to take leave till midnight, we sail at forenoon. Please pass that to the rest of the Squadron. Now shall we go to St Anne's and have some lunch?"

"Excellent idea, Commodore." Alf smiled.

The time was 0700, Commodore Alan Lee was having his morning bath, he could hear Timmins, setting the table for breakfast, and around him the distinctive sounds of a ship preparing to get underway. The bath shook a little as the ship's Engineer, let a small amount of steam into the turbines, to test them, all was well. Getting out of the bath, he dried and dressed quickly.

The ship's day had begun, 0715, the pipe 'Call the hands'; 0730 'Duty part of watch' wash down; 0745 hands to breakfast; 0800, colours; 0815, hands fall in for leaving the harbour, Special Sea duty men fall in, the familiar sounds heard on any Royal Navy ship the world over.

His freshly starched uniform would soon be soaked in sweat, but for a brief moment he looked smart. He finished his breakfast of eggs on toast, with a cup of tea. When his telephone rang, a distant voice spoke, "Commodore, OOW here, Captain said to tell you we are about to get underway."

"Very good, I will be up shortly." The phone clicked off. He waited ten minutes before making his way to the Bridge, after all, *Bristol*'s Captain would not like the Commodore on the bridge for departure. Closing his cabin door, the familiar Royal Marine Sentry stood at attention.

"Ah, Bennett, I see you have been demoted again?" Lee smiled.

"Wasn't my fault, sir, some Pongos were calling the *Bristol*, sir, couldn't let that happen, now could I!"

Lee shook his head. "You're a rascal, Bennett, but glad you are my rascal!" They both smiled. With men like this, how could we lose the war? He headed towards the bridge; the dawn appearing over the St Angelo battlements. The ship slowly gathering weight, the Tannoy sprung into life.

"Attention on the upper deck turn to port and salute C-in-C Malta."

What a difference from the past few visits, when they had to leave Malta, with all guns manned and in action, how things had changed for the better. Standing quietly at the rear of the bridge, Lee watched with satisfaction as the ship's company went about their business, the whispered orders, all calm. The Chief Buffer spotted Lee. "Commodore on the bridge," and the crew all stiffened up to salute him.

"Carry on," he spoke. As they approached the breakwater, Lee looked to starboard, and could just make out the abandoned wreck of the tanker *Ohio*, resting on the sea bed her back broken, and his mind went back to that day in Aug '42, when they brought it in, which helped to save Malta, and at the cost of his beloved *Preston*!

Swept out of the harbour by two *Bangor* class minesweepers, three of his Destroyers fanned out as an Anti-submarine screen, then followed *Bristol*, the carriers and then the rest of his force. They headed north then north by east. Increasing speed to sixteen knots, they were going back to war. As soon as they had enough wind over the decks, the carriers started to launch search aircraft and a combat air patrol over his force. Lost aircraft and crews had been replaced from the Royal Navy stocks at Hal Far airfield, so the Squadron was back up to full strength. Also, *Fencer* had arrived with a deck park of Hellcat fighters, clearly somebody had listened to him. The Seafires and Barracuda bombers had been replaced by all Hellcats, these would take over the roles of fighter and dive bombers. It was an experiment to see how it would work. But clearly all were happy with the arrangements.

After the attack on Taranto, the Italian navy dispersed the remaining ships further north into the Adriatic. As the Allied armies headed north up the length of Italy, it was becoming increasingly obvious that there was going to be nowhere to hide very soon. As the 30th Aircraft Carrier Squadron headed north, armed strike aircraft roamed at will, attacking everything that floated. Coasters, Luggers, trawlers, and small escort vessels, all felt the heavy hand of the Royal Navy. As they approached Bari, a small convoy of coastal vessels escorted by two *VP* boats, was spotted rushing to get into Bari harbour. The Avenger and Hellcat strike force fell on them with glee. After thirty minutes all five coasters and the two *VP* boats were all sunk. Unfortunately, the Germans had repositioned some of its fighter squadrons further south. A *Luftwaffe* detachment fell on the strike force, and in the wild melee of twisting and turning aircraft, three Avengers and two Hellcats were lost. Two Walrus SAR aircraft headed to the scene to look for survivors. There was a miscommunication, and the SAR defending fighter escort turned up late. Too late to help the lumbering Walrus, the enemy Fw 190s chewed them to bits. On the bridge of *Bristol*, it was a very angry Commodore Lee, when he found out about the loss of his Walrus and crews!

Another strike force of aircraft was sent east, to the ancient Yugoslav town of Dubrovnik and its port Gruz. Lee gave instructions that damage to the town was to be avoided at all costs. He did not want to be held responsible for damage to this magnificent town. Again a few small coasters and an ancient Yugoslav warship were sunk, with no loss to his force. It had been reported that there was a lot of coastal traffic in and around the islands between Dubrovnik and Pula. The force headed further north. A detachment of two Destroyers and two Cruisers were sent to investigate. The carriers launched further strikes on the islands. Yet again they crisscrossed the area sinking many small craft. The naval Strike force sunk a medium-sized merchant ship and an escorting warship. They did come under attack by a force of *Kreigsmarine* E-*Boats*, based at Šolta. A further strike force of Hellcats was sent to attack the base. The small aerodrome at Bisom had recently received ten Me 109 fighters. When the Hellcats strike force was spotted, eight of the 109s managed to get airborne and tested their skills with the Fleet Air Arm pilots. The bulk of the German pilots were fresh out of flight training. The highly trained and experienced Hellcat Pilots made short work of them, all being shot down. Unknown to the Navy pilots, a large group of AA guns had been set up surrounding the harbour, and two *Flak Lighters* had been positioned within the harbour. The sky over Šolta erupted in black exploding shells and tracer rounds reached for the attacking Hellcats. For thirty minutes the *Flak* gunners kept up a tremendous barrage. Four Hellcats succumbed to the fire; three others retired with significant damage. When the strike force withdrew, one *Flak Lighter* had sunk, the other was burning, and three E-*Boats* were destroyed. The Royal Navy would be back. As evening descended, the aircraft returned to their carriers, once onboard they retired to the mid-Adriatic to take stock and rest. The next morning, they would return to Šolta in much greater force.

9 Death of a Flotilla

Sat at his desk, at Hotel Flamingo, Kapitän zur See Kleber, shirt open to the waist, was sweating badly. This made him more irritable than usual. Behind his back, his men used the nickname Brummbär (Grouch).

His mind went back to the happy times, when he commissioned the 7th Flotilla, at Cuxhaven on the North Sea, in the heady days when the German Forces were spreading unrelentingly across Europe. It had been a pleasure cruise, bringing his ten E-*Boats* down from the cold North Sea to the warmth of the Mediterranean. Leaving Cuxhaven, they proceeded to Rotterdam, from there they entered the Rhine River, then onward to Strasbourg. Along the way, enthusiastic crowds cheered and waved, passing onboard fresh bread and wine. From there they entered the Rhine – Rhone Canal. Traversing the one-hundred-and-sixty-seven locks, they proceeded to the Belfort Gap at Lyon. Down the river until it met the Vouges Mountains then west to the Soane and the Border with Vichy France. From there they entered the river Rhone, which they followed until they reached Marscillcs. From then on it had been relentless, escorting Italian convoys, and launching torpedo attacks on British convoys. Sneaking around Malta laying mines, dropping secret agents off behind enemy lines in North Africa. The

Kriegsmarine and Luftwaffe had reigned supreme. All that had changed, the enemy now had the upper hand. Forced back by relentless pressure his remaining boats had fought a stiff rear-guard action, as they retreated up the length of the Adriatic Sea. He was desperately short of everything, men, spares, fuel, and ammunition, but most the time, he needed time to rest his men and refit his remaining boats.

Kriegsmarine Headquarters in Berlin never stopped demanding lists, on ammunition and fuel used, spares, and staff changes; it went on and on. Did those fools not know there was a war on? His head jerked up as the air raid siren started its mournful wail, standing up he went to the door as the first aircraft streaked across the harbour, its guns spitting out death. The lighter guns around the harbour started firing, followed by the deeper thump of the heavier weapons. Soon the air was filled with exploding shells, their black clouds darkening the sky, and enemy aircraft streaked in and out spreading destruction and death. Then, as quickly as it started, it was all over; he ran down to the harbour to assess the damage. One Flak lighter was sinking, the other one on fire, and eight small traders and small launches were either sunk or on fire. Worst of all, three of his remaining E-*Boats* were destroyed. Burning ammunition exploding with a crackle and pop, until the waters of the harbour extinguished them. Quickly giving his orders, Kleber realized that this location would have to be abandoned, and his remaining four boats moved further north. His men worked through the day loading all remaining spares onboard the four boats, the sick and wounded were brought on board and the force prepared for a dawn departure. Equipment that could not be loaded, was destroyed as his men went on a destructive rampage around the small town. An abandoned Italian MAS boat was acquired, and this was loaded with anything of value.

Standing on the bridge of 'his' boat, S-121, his hand resting on the scared woodwork around the armoured bridge, he felt, then heard the rumble of the three Mercedes-Benz diesel engines as they coughed into life. He looked with fondness at his crew as they went about their business, it had been a pleasure to lead these men, what a pity they had been let down by people higher up in command. However, it was time to go. Looking across the jetty, he watched as the other four Captains put their hand in the air, to say they were ready. With a nod, they cast off the bow and stern line, and quietly headed for the entrance. S-121 leading, followed by S-124, S-125, S-129 and finally the MAS boat M-566. It was a beautiful Mediterranean dawn as a blood red sun crept above the horizon, the dark sky changing to a deep blue, and with a gentle breeze. S-121 cleared the harbour and increased speed. With a loud roar, four Hellcats in line abreast streaked around the headland, their wing sparkling as their guns opened fire together. Jamming the boat throttles forward 121 sluggishly picked up speed, the tired engines and the overloaded condition of the vessel did not help her. Multiple fifty caliber bullets tore into the boat, spare depth charges stowed on the stern were hit by explosive and incendiary bullets, and 121 disappeared in a terrific explosion. The three remaining E-*Boats* fared no better, trapped in the harbour, because of 121 blocking it, they had nowhere to go, and like fish in a barrel, the Hellcats sank them one by one. The MAS had been spared at the moment of departure, her engines failed, so she was by the jetty, in deep shadow.

As they headed towards the island of Šolta, the night was pitch black, the flight leader checked his compass and stopwatch, the island should show up straight ahead in about thirty minutes. He looked on either side of his aircraft, the soft light from the various aircraft instrument panels, and the flickering, blue exhaust gas flames clearly visible. All the aircraft were rising and falling as their wings bit into the cool night air. The sky started to lighten, and as the darkness slowly disappeared, Park, the flight leader, gave the signal to arm and test their weapons, a short flash and the faint sound of bullets being fired entered his cockpit. Another hand signal, and his force divided into two sections. He led his section down and to the right, and headed for the headland, that would lead to the entrance of the small harbour. The other group of aircraft headed inland towards the airfield.

In two groups of four aircraft, in line abreast, they streaked across the breakwater, they spotted the enemy E-*Boats* beginning to depart, and in an orderly attack, swooped on the boats with concentrated gunfire, the high explosive and incendiary shells tearing apart each boat. The other four aircraft followed up and attacked anything the first strike missed. They all then climbed to about five thousand feet and dived back down shooting at gun positions and military targets. The other twelve Hellcats, struck at the airfield from different directions, after multiple attacks, nothing of any military value remained undamaged, as smoke and dust spread across the shattered airfield. They proceeded across the island in an orgy of ground attack destruction at very low level. Once finished, they climbed high over the island and awaited their comrades to join them. The remaining aircraft tore across the island firing at anything of value, buildings, transport, the airfield, and harbour installations. As they headed South back to the carriers, the Flight Leader looked at his strike aircraft; he could not believe it, none were lost.

Now they were all back together, they headed for carriers, the adrenalin slowly leaving their bodies, weariness took over. Some pilots were struggling to stay awake. As they neared the carrier's position, Park could see AA shell bursts over the top of the carriers. Aircraft were spotted diving down to attack. Other Hellcats were involved in deadly aerial dogfights. He ordered his fighters to make more height, then swooped down on the attacking German bombers. Within moments the sky was clear of enemies, as the remaining Germans headed back to Italy. It was clear that *Ruler* had been struck, as smoke was coming from her aft aircraft lift, and *Cleopatra* was turning in a tight circle, also billowing smoke. More fighters were being launched to provide aerial cover as the defending fighters and the strike aircraft landed back on their carriers, *Ruler*'s aircraft landed wherever they could.

At four o'clock in the morning, *Striker* and *Ruler* turned into the wind, increased speed, and began launching the strike aircraft for the attack on Šolta. Once this was accomplished, they slowed down and continued north.

Unseen, they were being watched, the Italian Submarine *Italia II* was following them. Unable to get close for a Torpedo attack, because the escorting destroyers were very active. The sub-captain sent a message to the Italian Naval HQ, informing them of the carrier's position, course and speed. Nearing daybreak, *Italia II* had to leave, heading back to Taranto for fuel. At *Regia Marina HQ*, *Italia II*'s message was swiftly passed on to the *Regia Aeronautica,* and *Luftwaffe*. With remarkable efficiency, a large bomber force was assembled from various airfields on the East side of Italy and ordered into the attack.

Onboard the 30th ACS, dawn was breaking, and another flying day began, with the main strike launched, four fighters were sent aloft for a Combat Patrol overhead and four search aircraft were sent out to scout around. The ships then continued with normal duties, as they waited for the Strike force to return. Heading due west, *Nabob*'s Avenger aircraft '*Nora* 07', climbed above a large cloud formation, the pilot having no intention of flying through it unless he had to; it might look white and fluffy on the outside, but he knew it was as black as pitch on the inside and had dangerous high winds. As he cleared the cloud, he spotted a large formation of bomber aircraft heading east, they could only be going in one direction, 'The Fleet'.

"Sparks get on the box, plain language, many bombers heading your way, quick as you can." The message was never received by the carriers, *Nora 07*'s radio was not working. So, he then deliberately headed into the cloud bank, he would follow the enemy aircraft and continue to send reports, in the hope the carriers heard it. The radar onboard *Bristol* picked up the incoming raid. The alarm rattlers sounded for action stations, and all four carriers headed into the wind to launch fighters. The next fifteen minutes were taken up with the boom of anti-aircraft fire, tracer bullets crisscrossing the sky, empty brass shell casings clattering onto steel decks, the scream of dive bombers and the crump of exploding bombs. *Cleopatra* was singled out for particular attention. Hit by two bombs her steering room was damaged, which left her in a tight turning circle. A third bomb hit by the side of her forward multiple Bofors gun, killing or wounding her entire gun crew. Unfortunately, as the gun captain slumped forward, his body jammed against the gun firing control. As *Cleopatra* continued to turn, *Ruler* appeared across the front of the Bofors gun barrels. A stream of forty-millimetre shells smashed into *Ruler*'s bridge structure, and swept across the flight deck, setting fire to various aircraft parked there and decimating the flight deck crew. As the ammunition bins on the Bofors went empty, there was a shocked silence onboard the ships of the force. By this time the surviving enemy aircraft were in full retreat, leaving the immediate sky to the defending fighters. The well-drilled damage control teams swung into action. *Stinger* went alongside *Ruler* and played water hoses onto the burning flight deck. *Savage* joined *Cleopatra,* also to assist in firefighting.

Lee was shocked, yet again his command had been hurt badly. All through the rest of the day, the clear-up continued, ammunition lockers were restocked, and action repairs were carried out. On *Ruler*, fresh flight deck planking was laid. Destroyed aircraft were unceremoniously dumped overboard, and fresh aircraft were brought into action. *Cleopatra*'s steering was repaired and the fire was out. By evening the force was ready again to fight. They headed north again, into the night, and a sombre mood descended on the ships. With the dawn, again brought the sound of aircraft engines, as the duty carrier readied her Search and Combat Patrol aircraft ready for another day of action. The plan was to scout out Ancona in Italy and Zadar in Yugoslavia, for a strike later in the day. An hour after dawn, the ship's radar plots reported another wave of enemy aircraft approaching from the west.

10 Adriatic Finale

Sat in his cabin, on board *Hermes*, the high summer heat was oppressive. He took another drink from his Schappes bottle, after all, there was nothing else to do! He would visit his Italian girlfriend after the sun went down for another night of mechanical sex, and he was starting to tire of her. Korvette Kaptain Johan Rindt was awaiting orders from the German Naval command in Rome. He had taken over *Hermes* about eighteen months ago. A captured Greek Destroyer, that had been built by the British, and he had sailed far and wide in the Mediterranean Sea, causing chaos to the enemy. Credited with sinking a British destroyer, two submarines, and multiple coastal supply ships up and down the African coast. He also conducted a daring attack on a convoy of merchantmen sailing from Alexandria to Malta, sinking two ships, before having to retreat under heavy fire. Now his command was tied up at the *M*olo Audace in the harbour of *Trieste*, covered from stem to stern by camouflage netting. He was trapped here, his ship needed a refit, he only had half-full fuel bunkers, and his ammunition stocks were low. He could go nowhere. He guessed the 'Grand Scheme' would be to make a one-way trip to attack the Allies, cause as much damage as he could and get himself sunk. Not a prospect he was looking forward to. His men deserved better. The damn Italians wouldn't refuel him, and the engineers for his refit had suddenly disappeared. So, he sat and drank Schnapps. He stood up, jammed his cap on his head, and made his way onto the deck. The British had built this ship well, and he was very happy to command it, and being Royal Navy, he had two cabins, one, near the bridge, and a second, bigger one at the stern, which he now spent much of his time in. As he stood on the deck, he watched his crew as they went about doing essential maintenance, but in this heat, there was not much enthusiasm. He moved and stood by the ship's rail. He watched as two Italian MAS boats left the pier Molo IV and headed out to sea, their engines leaving a low growling noise as they increased speed. A voice next to him shook from his reverie.

"Herr Kapitän, message for you." The signalman saluted smartly and proffered him a signal pad.

"Thanks, Karl, let's see what they want now?"

Rindt's orders were simple; sail at midnight, in company with two *Vp* boats and the three *MAS* boats and attack the Allied aircraft carriers in the Adriatic. The Italian navy had been ordered to top up his fuel tanks, and a small coaster was due any moment with captured ammunition for his main four-point-seven-inch guns and one torpedo. He was then, to return to Trieste and await further orders. If he survived, he thought. Shortly a small fuel tanker came alongside and started topping up his tanks. The two MAS boats that had left earlier, returned with a small coasting vessel. This was also tied up alongside and precious ammunition was loaded onboard. The two *VP* boat Captains were ordered to come aboard, and he asked them to ignore their orders; armed Trawlers had no place in the upcoming engagement. He asked them to sail later and help with rescue operations, they would be of more use to him then! The Captains agreed, and with a relieved smile said their goodbyes. At midnight, the three *MAS* boats, made their way out of Trieste Harbour, followed by *Hermes*. They turned and headed south. The Torpedo boats spread out in a broad front. Having been unable to do any repairs, *Hermes* struggled on behind at a maximum of twenty-four knots; he would be at a tactical disadvantage.

Onboard *Bristol*, Lee watched as his Hellcat fighters clawed for height, as they headed for the next incoming air raid. The first raid of the morning had caused little damage, fourteen enemy aircraft had been shot down by his fighters, now this second raid was approaching. It was noticeable that there were fewer enemy aircraft in each succeeding raid. He wondered if his orders to draw off the enemy aircraft were working. However, after his planned strike on Zadar and Ancona, he would have to again retire to Malta for refuelling and restocking ammunition. He watched the bridge radar repeater, as his aircraft ripped into the attacking enemy. It didn't last long, another twelve enemy aircraft crashed into the sea, and the rest retired, gallantly, at great speed for the Italian coast. The cost was two more Hellcat fighters, but both pilots were rescued. Before his fighters landed, he launched his two-strike forces for the attack on Zadar and Ancona. Every available aircraft headed to the targets, his remaining twelve fighters landed for fuel, while six fighters took over the aerial protection of the fleet.

The two aerial strikes fell upon the targeted towns, the damage included the docks being badly damaged, a total of five coastal vessels sunk, along with an armed trawler and two medium-sized freighters. The airfields were strafed until nothing of any value was left. Burning aircraft wrecks littered the airfields.

Around lunchtime, Lee retired to his cabin to eat and compose a message for the Admiralty to update and instruct them on his next actions. Above his head, the alarm rattlers sounded off. The sound of seaboots running across the deck, as the Tannoy sounded "Action station, enemy ships in sight, stand by surface action". Grabbing his steel helmet, he launched himself across the cabin, scattering his meal and paperwork in all directions. He fell against a bulkhead as the ship turned hard a port, and the 'Y' gun above his head opened fire, the concussion pinning him to the deck. He eventually arrived on the bridge covered in paint chips, smelling of cordite fumes and with his ears ringing. Without instructions, Matley had ordered the Carriers to head south at maximum speed, Smoke belching from their funnels, escorted by *Fernie*, *Silverton*, *Napier*, *Nepal*, *and Cleopatra*. The remaining warships formed a line on *Bristol* as they interdicted themselves to shield the carriers.

In the 'B' turret, L/S Sam Holt took his seat in between two of the three-gun barrels, it was cramped in there. He looked over his right shoulder and he could just make out his mate, Dan Moore, as he stood by the fuze setter, he looked scared, and Holt gave him a wink. 'Load, Load, Load' came over the Tannoy, behind him three six inch shells slid forward from the loading trays, forced by the hydraulic rammer into the gaping hole of the gun breech. The rammers withdrew and three bags of Cordite, dropped into the loading trays, and these were also rammed into the breech, one each gun, with a hiss the rammer retracted and the loading trays folded out of reach, as the barrel was sealed by the breech block as it pivoted into position. The range and bearing of the enemy ships was fed into the gun layer and aimers headsets. Holt turned his training gear as he peered through his gun site to spot the enemy. Once he was happy, he would call out, "Layer on," followed by his opposite number who shouted "Aimer on," the Gun Captain spoke on the telephone, "'B' gun ready!" The order, 'Shoot', was heard followed by the ting-ting of the firing bell. Left and right barrels slammed back into their recoil springs, followed a split second later by the centre barrel. The noise was terrific, clouds of dust flew into the air from every nook and cranny, and the turret lighting flickered. The gun breeches opened, and three spent brass cartridge cases fell on the turret floor and a puff of high-pressure air was discharged into the gun barrel to clear the gases from the firing, the sequence would start again, loading trays came into position, shells, loaded, rammed, cordite loaded and rammed, and the ting-ting again, as the crews' senses were assaulted by the noise and blast from the guns. By the fourth salvo, they suffered a misfire. The drill was to extract the round, throw it overboard, wait thirty minutes, then reload, and commence firing again. Of course, that was never going to happen! Six crew members struggled with the one-hundred-and-twenty-pound shell, to get it out of the turret and throw it overboard, reloaded and commenced firing again within six minutes.

In what seemed like a very short time later, the cease fire gong went off. They had fired thirty full salvoes at the enemy force. Now the adrenalin stopped flowing, and their bodies started to relax; people were giddy, sleepy, angry, all the emotions that could affect the human body. Holt looked at his mate and smiled and gave the 'thumbs up' they lived for another day. Now they had to clean up the turret and replace the ready use ammunition, before they were stood down.

"Report," asked Lee. Matley quickly filled in what had occurred, and Lee agreed with everything.

"Alf, how did they get so close before being spotted?" Lee asked.

"My fault, sir, I was watching for aircraft, and these ships approached under cover of a fog bank. We have three torpedo boats and a destroyer attacking." They watched as the Hellcats that were airborne pounced on the MAS boats, their point five-inch machine gun bullets ripping the wooden boats to shreds. The warships concentrated fire on *Hermes*.

Looking through his binoculars, Lee spoke, "I've seen that destroyer before, she attacked my force near Malta months ago, she's ex-Greek, taken over by the Germans." Soon, she was a burning wreck, pummelled by British high explosive, and armoured piercing shells. She did not last long. Her bow raised towards the sky, as she slowly sank below the waves.

On *Hermes*, Rindt thought he had caught the Britishers napping. They had not spotted his force as it closed, using the fog bank as cover. Ordering the Torpedo boats forward to start an immediate torpedo attack, *Hermes* turned to starboard to try and close the range so he could use this last torpedo. Shortly after leaving the fog bank, the airborne fighters spotted the MAS boats, and like avenging angels fell upon the lightly armed boats with a vengeance. He watched as they lined up and strafed them into burning hulks, the crews trying to escape the onslaught by jumping overboard. It did not last long. As he watched, three huge brown water columns rose on either side of his *Hermes*, that large cruiser had opened fire! Twisting and turning, he tried to avoid the enemy shells, but it was one-sided. A hit amidships on the single torpedo warhead caused massive damage to the second boiler room and the forward engine room. Soon his speed was dropping significantly, and as the range dropped, his command was being hit regularly. It was time to abandon the ship, he ordered, as he turned to leave the bridge, he was blown to bits, as a high explosive six-inch shell smashed into the conning position. The sea was soon littered with floating flotsam, and men struggling in the water as the four Axis warships sank. Much later as the two *VP* Boats arrived on the scene, there were very few survivors. High above, a lone Italian SM79 watched as the enemy retired, and he could see his comrades struggling in the water below.

As his force reformed and his aircraft recovered, Lee ordered a return to Malta. On the way south he received a top-secret message from the Admiralty, the landings in Southern France had been a great success, with little aerial opposition. Also, congratulations on his success in the Adriatic. The four carriers, because of the congestion in the Grand Harbour, were detached to anchor in Marsaxlokk harbour. The rest entered the Grand Harbour, with a broom tied to every main mast, to show they had swept the seas of the enemy. They received a raptures welcome from the people of Malta. The next week was spent giving the crews leave, restocking and repairs, all with assistance from the dockyard, which was now getting back to full operation.

11 Aegean

Eight days later, they were back to sea, his force was now joined by his supply ships. Their destination was the Aegean Sea. The first task was to get the new pilots up to combat ready, so a series of exercises were conducted to assist them. Refuelling at sea was also practiced, an evolution that his ships desperately needed to get back up to speed on. Commodore Lee watched from the flagship, making sure he missed nothing, the good and the bad! If all went well a 'manoeuvere well executed' was passed the appropriate ship, if not, a stinging signal was sent to all involved. He had lost the two 'Hunts', they had returned to Gibraltar, and he was very sad to see them go. Before departure, he boarded both ships, 'cleared lower deck' and thanked them for their efforts, a gesture that went down well.

ACS 30's new orders were to enter the Aegean and to support the invasion of some of the islands in the Dodecanes. Yet another one of Churchill's hair-brain ideas! The plan was to invade the strategic islands of Rhodes, Crete, Kithira, Cos, Leros and the Cyclades. However, Eisenhower, the supreme allied commander had other ideas and wanted no disseveration of his forces, which would be desperately needed for the upcoming D-Day landings. So, Churchill ordered the available forces from the Middle East to be assembled and with the Royal Navy and Royal Air Force's aid to capture these islands. However, it was a pitifully small force that could be raised, and they suffered appalling casualties. Lee's force was sent in to provide some support and respite, for the exhausted allied troops. Of all the RAF Squadrons involved, the two Spitfire squadrons had been decimated and had only three serviceable aircraft left, the Halifax and Dakota squadrons fared no better.

Lee planned to approach the island of Crete from the south, if he was to enter the Aegean, he needed to eliminate any enemy air opposition on Crete. He did not want anything to surprise his forces from the rear. Speaking with his Senior Pilots, they came up with a plan of action. This was going to be a maximum strike; every available aircraft would be launched. The bulk of the Avengers would attack the airfield at Maleme and Heraklion, approaching from east and west. Ten Hellcat fighter bombers, from *Fencer*, would attack the small airfield on the south coast at Mythos, twelve Hellcats would serve as a Combat Air Patrol over the top of the strike aircraft and eight aircraft would do the same for the carriers. After the strike, all aircraft had instructions to strike targets of opportunity on the way back to the carriers. But on no account to attack the local population! Again, the Walrus aircraft would be committed to Search and Rescue, but this time they had an escort of four fighters, that lesson had been well learnt!

Dawn found the carriers thirty miles south of Crete, just out of sight of land. The air was full of the sound of radial engines coughing into life, the air above each carrier was hazy, with the blue exhaust gases, from each aircraft as the crew prepared for the mass take-off. First to go was the fighter protection for the fleet, then the strike force, the heavily laden Avengers using the catapults to get airborne as the carriers steamed at full speed to get some wind over the decks, the winds being very light and variable. The first few aircraft struggled to get airborne as the big radial engines clawed at the thin hot air to gain height and airspeed. When all the aircraft had departed, the only sounds were the hiss of the sea, the gentle hum of the engine room fans, and the quiet conversations of the crew, the scrape of a seaboot across a grating. Above their heads the radar antennas searched the skies, behind him, the DCT turned gently on its roller bed, the crew checking the distant horizon for enemies. Lee sat in his chair, content with the stillness of the early morning. He sipped his cup of coffee, as his mind went back a couple of years, he was back in this area, where the pride of the Mediterranean Fleet was decimated by the Luftwaffe. The scream of the diving Stuka's, and the crump of exploding bombs, was still ringing in his ears, so many ships, so many men, all now at rest on the sea bed beneath their feet. Now, it was time for revenge. Across the bridge, Matley watched his friend, he knew what Lee was thinking, he could see the pain etched across his face. The phone next to him buzzed, another problem in the engine room, the Captain's job never ending!

High above the mountains of Crete, The Senior Pilot, Miles Davies, looked on either side of his windscreen, the strike aircraft rose and fell gently from the warm updrafts from the mountains below. His mission was the airfield at Heraklion, and the flying boats anchored in Suda Bay. His pilots needed little instruction, they were now well trained and combat tested, mounted in superb American aircraft, and they feared no one. Nodding to his next in command, and with a hand signal, six Hellcats broke away and headed for Suda Bay, which he could just make out in the dawn mists. His Avengers broke into two groups and headed for the airfield from east and west. His fighters would attack from south to north, a tactic he had used before. This allowed for different directions for attack and caused maximum damage and lessoned the risk to his crews, as only one attacking pass was needed. Moments later, over the radio he ordered the attack. Ahead, above the airfield, the sky blossomed into black clouds as the anti-aircraft gunners woke up.

The other strike force, led by Lt Mike Keary, another red-haired Irishman from Belfast, a superb pilot, and excellent leader when airborne, but a fire-eating maniac on the ground. His disciplinary record was poor! He looked down at the airfield at Maleme. Splitting his forces like Davies's they attacked from three sides. As he headed down, he was aware of many wrecked Ju52 aircraft scattered around the airfield perimeter. The legacy of the airborne assault when the Germans took the airfield. He spotted two of his fighters attacking these wrecks, quickly speaking on the radio, he ordered them to shift targets. Unfortunately, it was too late for one of the fighters as it was ripped apart by a concealed twenty-millimetre gun mounting. It sank to the ground, hit a ditch and then cartwheeled across the runway in a huge funeral pyre.

Over Heraklion, Davis pulled on his joystick, his aircraft zoomed skywards, at twenty-thousand feet he levelled out and looked down at the battered airfield. The paved runway was cratered, three aircraft hangers were ablaze, and multiple aircraft were wrecked or on fire around the perimeter, for the cost of one Avenger damaged and at this moment was struggling back to the carrier with a fighter escort. Looking across at Suda Bay he could just see the broken wreck of the Heavy Cruiser *H.M.S. York*, sunk there many months before. Also seven funeral pyres, all that remained of the enemy aircraft that had been stationed there. The southern strike force had obliterated the few aircraft on the airstrip at Mythos, they now circled above the returning aircraft and followed them back to the carriers. On his left side, he could just make out Keary's force heading back to join up with his. Davis counted the number of returning aircraft; two fighters were missing and two Avengers showing signs of battle damage, if that was all, they had achieved another victory!

A follow-up strike was organised for later that day, this time, just Hellcats would be used. Again, very little opposition was noted, and no losses amongst the carrier aircraft. Anything of military value, that was missed the first time, did not survive the second attack. Well contented, Lee turned the force to the south, he wanted to get some sea room, so he could top up supplies from his store ships. All went well apart from a broken oil fuel line from the tanker *Olna* to *Scorpion*. That wasted most of the following morning as repairs were carried out. They then headed further north into the Aegean Sea.

The first target was the island of Rhodes, the largest of the Dodecanese islands. Following the fall of Greece, it was occupied by the Italians. The principal airport at Maritsa would be the first target, again a coordinated attack from multiple directions by Bombers and Fighters, after which shipping in the port of Rhodes was to be the target. Intelligence had told them that there was a strong force of German aircraft stationed there, and they had to be eliminated first. At 0430, about thirty-five miles due south of the island, the carriers turned into the wind and started launching aircraft. Onboard *Striker*, the Hellcats took off one by one. The first Avenger was catapulted into the air successfully, as the second aircraft was being positioned, a hydraulic pipe burst, spewing hot fluid all across the deck. This caused the following take-offs to be stopped. Engineers and artificers scrambled across *Striker*'s flight deck, ripping up planking to locate and repair the offending pipe. Onboard *Nabob*, a similar event occurred, fortunately as the last Avenger was being launched. This aircraft did not have enough airspeed to get airborne; as it staggered off the bow, it sank out of sight and plunged into the sea. *Nabob* was slow to turn, and the ship ran over the unlucky aircraft, the entire aircrew being lost. *Nabob* was also very lucky as the four five-hundred-pound bombs on the stricken aircraft did not have time to arm themselves, so they descended to the sea bed safely. One of *Fencer*'s aircraft landed back onboard the ship safely with engine troubles. After the eventful few minutes, the depleted strike force formed up into its flights and headed North.

Lee ordered an immediate inspection on all four carriers, into the catapult failures. It soon came back; the pipework on, *Striker*, *Ruler* and *Nabob*, was showing signs of considerable corrosion. On *Fencer*, because the catapult had not been used much, the corrosion was not bad. The store's ship *Corinder*, had sufficient spare pipe to repair one ship. He had to make a decision, on what to do. Because the Avengers, when 'bombed up', needed the catapults' assistance to get airborne. The Hellcats, on a normal day, didn't need them. After consultation, it was decided to transfer all the Avengers to *Fencer*. *Fencer* would then send her fighters to *Striker*. *Ruler* would get the repairs, and *Nabob* would stop using bombers when the wind was light. It was the best solution to keep his ships on station and active.

Unaware of what was going on back at the fleet, the attacking aircraft split into three separate forces. With the signal from SPLOT, the aircraft commenced their attack. The enemy gunners were wide awake, and the sky above the airfield blossomed into black bursting anti-aircraft shells. The fighters dived down and commenced their low-level strike, while the Avengers climbed for altitude, to carry out a less risky high-level bombing attack. The Bomber pilots looked down as the fighters peeled away from the airfield, scattered around were the remains of burning Ju 88s and Me 109s caught on the ground. In a coordinated strike, all bombers opened their bomb doors together and deposited their loads of two-thousand pounds of high explosives in a carpet across the dispersal area. Dust and debris reached high into the air. The loss of another Avenger due to a technical issue was the only incident, and all aircrews returned safely to their carriers.

They then headed further into the Aegean; Recon aircraft were sent out to look for further targets. The ships took the opportunity to refuel. The following morning, the force turned into the wind and two strike forces were launched. One to the port and airfield of Naxos, the other towards Samos, where they split into two attacking forces, one for the small airfield at Potokaki and the other for the port of Samos, this being the more awkward as the port sits at the bottom of some very steep hills. Sat in his bridge chair, Lee was talking quietly to Matley. The phone rang next to Matley.

"Captain here."

A tinny voice spoke, "Radar plot, sir. Enemy aircraft approaching from the north. Thirty-plus aircraft."

"Action Stations, air raid red!" Lee watched as *Nabob* and *Fencer* turned into the wind and started launching fighter aircraft. Onboard *Bristol*, the gun crews took up their action stations efficiently.

It was a mixed bag of aircraft that the Germans had been gathered together to attack the 30th ACS. None of them could be classed as front-line machines. *Nabob* and *Fencer*'s fighters fell upon them with a will, for some of the fighter pilots it was uncomfortable viewing, the enemy were simply eliminated! These were very inexperienced pilots. Soon the attacking force was either a smoking wreck or had fled for home. There was not much celebrations amongst the victorious Allied pilots. The attack force also found little enemy air activity as they attacked the target islands of Samos and Naxos. However, the German anti-aircraft fire was a different story. Three Avengers and three Hellcats were badly damaged and barely made it back to the carriers. On the up side, four coasters were sunk in Naxos harbour, and some small craft in Samos harbour were also destroyed. The airfields were left as smouldering wrecks, the few second line and transport aircraft, there, totally destroyed.

With the collapse of the Italian government and their capitulation to the Allies, the German High Command moved swiftly to take over the islands of Cos (Kos), Leros, Samos and Rhodes. Lee's instructions were to interdict this invasion force and stop the occupation. Ordering a survey of the area, then he laid out his plans. Just like Crete a few years ago, the Germans were massing on Stampalia and Pseimos islands, and, just like the Crete invasion, were using local Caiques, VJ Boats and Siebel ferries and a few small coastal trading vessels to transport the crack troops of Lt. General Frederick Mueller's 22nd Infantry Division. As dawn broke, his Avengers and Hellcats fell on the enemy shipping. For an hour they ran riot, but then the German Luftwaffe arrived overhead, and a swirling, zooming dogfight ensued. These were not the tired clapped aircraft of the Italian theatre, these were battle-hardened squadrons, sent south from the Russian front, to assist in the invasion. An eight-strong Destroyer force led by the legendary warship *HMS Faulknor* came through the Straights, between Leros and Stampalia, and sank the shipping missed by the attacking aircraft. It was carnage, with hundreds of German soldiers left dead or struggling in the water. Relief fighters were scrambled to give cover as the destroyers, as they retired to the sanctuary of Turkish Territorial waters. From there they hugged the coast back to Cyprus for resupply and refuel.

Lee spoke to Davies, he was worried, the pilots were becoming tired and fatigued, they had been in action for weeks now, ever since the attack on *Tirpitz*, which seemed like years ago. This fell nicely into the Commodore's plans, he ordered that the force should retire to the south, and head for Alexandria, to rest the crew and give the dockyard in Alex. The opportunity to carry out proper repairs to the ship's catapults. A message was sent to the Admiralty and C-in-C Mediterranean fleet of his actions.

Four days later, as they passed through 'The Narrows' into Alexandria's harbour, *Bristol* suddenly shuddered, and a huge geyser of dirty brown water erupted abreast her starboard side near the propellor shafts. She had triggered a magnetic mine, laid by the Germans months ago and missed by the local minesweeping force. *Bristol* had been badly damaged. Matley and his crew quickly had the situation under control, and although listing badly, she was in no danger of sinking. Three tugs came out of Alexandria to assist *Bristol* into port, and prepared her to be placed in the floating dry dock.

The rest of the force stood off until the passage was swept again by the minesweepers and declared safe. Then they passed the breakwater into the home of the Eastern Mediterranean fleet. The two carriers, with the most urgent need, were quickly tied up to the shipyard wall, and just prior to arrival, all the serviceable aircraft had been flown off to the local FAA airfield for some well-needed repairs and upgrades, and lost aircraft were replaced with fresh new ones. Later, replacement pilots would join the squadrons.

Down south in the Durban dockyard, *HMS Stockport* was just being eased out of the dry dock, her lower hull having been scraped and repainted, and a long-standing leak in the port inner shaft was also repaired. The two tugs pushed and cajoled her alongside the dock wall, where the lorries and railway waggons stood waiting to restock the ship with all her needs. At the barracks just outside town, L/S De Asha his sidekick Jenkins and a few other hangers-on were packing up their belongings, ready for the move back onboard ship.

During the refit, it had been a profitable time for De Asha, having fallen in with the local smugglers and gangsters, and had managed to swop ship stores for items that would bring a large profit when he returned to the UK, like ivory, semi-precious stones, wood carvings, etc. All these had been secreted around the ship, away from prying eyes. The plan was for *Stockport* to return to the UK and decommission, then immediately recommission with a new crew and join the Home Fleet at Scapa Flow. The few remaining crew were looking forward to some time with their families. After a couple of days' hard work, the bulk of the stores were loaded, and it became obvious that the store assistants were becoming concerned at the large number of discrepancies in their lists. So, a muster was called and all hands were instructed to search the ship from keel to truck, in an attempt to find the missing stores. The hold flat was in the very bowels of the ship; surprisingly De Asha volunteered to take a section of men and search down there. The C.P.O. in charge was happy he had a volunteer, as this was part of the ship nobody wanted to search! After many hours of searching, the missing items could not be located. The First Lieutenant had to reluctantly 'write off' these items, at great cost to the ship. He would spend a great deal of his off-duty time searching the ship for the missing items.

"Do you hear there, this is the Acting Captain speaking, I know you were all looking forward to returning to Blighty, however, our plans have changed, we are sailing back to the Suez and Alexandria, (a large moan was heard) we are to rejoin Commodore Lee, as his flagship. Anybody with family issues please speak to your divisional Officers and we will see what we can do. That is all."

12 Bristol Despair

It was clear once *Bristol* had entered the dry dock that she was badly damaged. Her back was broken just aft of the engine room, it would take months of work just to make her watertight, so she could be floated out of the dock and sent to a major shipyard for repair, so a discussion had to be made about what to do!

Stockport, his old flagship, had just finished a refit in Durban, so she was ordered north to relieve *Bristol*. Lee, Matley and a few other key ratings would be transferred to *Stockport* and the mission could resume.

Two weeks later, the repairs to the carriers were completed, and the sun rose to find *HMS Stockport* at anchor in the harbour, taking on fuel and provisions. Andy Watson, *Stockport*'s temporary Captain would swop ships with Alf Matley and would standby *Bristol* while she was made ready for her trip home to Chatham for a full repair. Matley would be taking over *Stockport* for the next part of their orders.

Once refuelled, the force was led out by the destroyer *Savage*, turning to starboard, the other escorts fanning out to provide a security screen, they headed at twelve knots for the entrance to the Suez Canal, the next part of their mission. The squadrons were circling overhead, ready to commence landing back onboard their parent ship. It was a typical Mediterranean day, with clear blue skies, excellent visibility, and light winds. All went well until the last Avenger re-joining *Fencer*. On touch down, the arrester hook detached from the aircraft, and the unbridled aircraft proceeded across the deck, colliding with two parked Hellcats and disappeared overboard, taking its gallant young crew to their deaths, along with two brand new Hellcat fighters. The shock around the force was palpable, what a waste of brave men's lives, and much-needed aircraft. Lee ordered, in the time remaining before they entered the Suez, that all the aircraft and crews were to be launched to practice landings, he wanted no more repeats of that morning's episode.

At dawn the next day, they were in line astern, travelling at nine knots, again following *Savage* as they started their transit of the Canal. Ismailia, The Great Bitter Lakes, Little Bitter Lake, a route familiar to many sailors over the years. It takes sixteen hours for the force to reach the exit into the Red Sea.

The Commodore was sitting in his bridge chair, going through the latest batch of signals from the Admiralty. He was happy to see many familiar faces on the bridge around him. Matley was talking to *Stockport*'s First Lieutenant. The Chief Yeoman, Carrie, was stood at his side, Timmins, his steward, had just reached the bridge with a tray of sandwiches and a cup of coffee. Turning to look over his left shoulder, he could just see that scoundrel, De Asha, with his oppo Jenkins, quietly talking, and Marine Bennett, how had he made it onboard, he must ask Alf about that one. Still, all good hands and happy to command them all.

A young telegraphist passed a message 'flimsy' to Carrie, who with a quick glance passed it straight to Lee; it was marked Top Secret, eyes only.

He spoke, "How they doing Chief?"

Carrie sighed, "Not as good as *Bristol*'s but we are getting there, sir," and smiled.

Lee spoke, "Captain, would you and the Navigator join me in the chartroom, please?"

"Aye, sir."

The three officers stood around the chart table looking at a map of the north Indian Ocean. "Gentlemen, I have just received a message from 'Their Lordships', there is a German heavy Cruiser, loose in the Indian Ocean! She sank a tanker here (pointing to a point off Djibouti), which seems like a crazy place for a Heavy Cruiser to be, so close to Aden, and not much sea room to manoeuvre". They all looked at the map. "I will launch a maximum range scout, to have a look-see, but we are here, at the top of the Red Sea, and Eritrea is a long way south. Any ideas on where to look?"

On the bridge of the Kriegsmarine Heavy Cruiser *Seydlitz*, Kapitän zur See Hans Ludendorff looked at the chart. He was worried, he was running short of fuel, and had gambled on capturing a tanker in the Indian Ocean. His supply ship, *Sachsen*, had failed to make the last rendezvous, and he was becoming desperate, which is why he was so far north, close to the main British shipping lanes. The Norwegian tanker he captured yesterday, *Arctic,* had been loaded with crude oil, so was of no use to him. He put a prize crew onboard and ordered her to make for Germany, she would be a welcome addition to Germany's fuel stocks. Before she left, he ordered her wireless room to transmit a signal saying they were sinking, which might deceive the Allies for a while. Heading southeast, he headed in the direction of the Tanker traffic leaving the Gulf. He knew he had only a few more days of fuel remaining, so if he had no luck he would head towards Singapore and hand the ship over to the Japanese.

Three hundred miles of *Seydlitz*'s position, *Sachsen* rolled in the swell, the condensers in her boilers had failed. She was an old ship, and in the desperate times that the Third Reich was in, she had been ordered from her berth in Bordeaux to support the Heavy Cruiser. But she was not a naval auxiliary and little maintenance had been conducted in the last two years, but she was all that was available. So loaded with valuable fuel oil and with a scratch crew of Naval Ratings, she was sent out into the Atlantic. More by good luck than by any actions the crew took, she escaped any detection and even managed to rendezvous with *Seydlitz* on two occasions, and after initial problems, had made fuel transfers. Now heading north into the Indian Ocean for another meeting, she had spotted a patrolling British Cruiser, so putting her stern to the enemy she increased speed and disappeared over the horizon. Unfortunately, this was too much for her overworked boilers; first one, then a second boiler failed, so she had to continue north on just one boiler at an excruciating six knots as the engineers struggled to repair the unfamiliar equipment on the ship. Now, as they rebuilt boiler number one, the last boiler gave up the unequal struggle and with a loud sigh and hissing the remaining steam escaped through the safety valve. After struggling for two days on repairs, *Sachsen*'s Captain, Johan Forger, had no choice but to transmit his position to *Seydlitz* and to ask for help.

Onboard *Seydlitz*, the signal came like a bolt of lightning. Ludendorff headed for the chart table to plot a course to the stricken tanker. Once happy with the decision, he altered course and at an economical speed headed towards *Sachsen*.

In a nondescript warehouse in Dar es Salem, a small group of British Naval Intelligence officers eagerly decrypted the German Message, and a signal was soon rushing through the ether to a ramshackle house in Buckinghamshire.

Onboard *Stockport*, the order was given, south, at the carrier's maximum speed of sixteen knots. Two search aircraft had been sent out but with little chance of contact. He also ordered from Aden three Catalina Flying Boats to search to the south, also from Mombasa two Sunderlands were ordered to search to the east. All Lee could do now was to wait, while the Flyboys did their jobs. Sat in his chair on the bridge, the sun blazed down, he pulled his cap down lower over his eyes to shade them from the fierce sun. The heat was terrific, thank goodness they had wind wafting over ships. He picked up the engine room phone and spoke to Ray Arnold, enquiring about the heat below decks and the fuel situation. Content with the answers, he put the phone down just as Timmins, his faithful servant, showed up on the bridge with a jug of lemonade and a sandwich! "Ah bless you, Timmins."

Chief Yeoman Carrie walked out of the signal office and made his way to Lee's chair. He noted the Commodore was in a light-hearted conversation with the Skipper.

"Excuse me, sir, priority message for you from the Admiralty," he said and handed the 'flimsy' for Lee to look at.

Lee raised his voice, "Captain, can you and the Pilot join me in the chart room please?"

"Sir."

As they headed down the Red Sea, Lee spoke to the SPLOT on the TBS, "Hi Miles, fresh orders, we are to search the southern Gulf of Aden for a crippled German Tanker and the Heavy Cruiser *Seydlitz*, Their Lordships think they are about three hundred miles east of Somalia. As soon as we get near the exit of the Red, I want a maximum search programme, link it in with Aden and Mombasa's aircraft." Due to the atmospheric conditions the static over the TBS was quite bad, so it took some time for the message to get through.

"Understood, sir, I will work it out and let you know soonest."

"Thanks, Miles. How are your airmen doing, have they been resting and ready to go?"

"Yes, sir, ready to go."

"OK, Miles, leave it with you. Father out."

With little fuel remaining, it was a relief for Ludendorff when *Sachsen* moved into view, his priority was to fill his tanks. However, this is not an easy manoeuvre to undertake with the pitch and roll of the ship not under control. But by passing a wire and a hose astern of *Sachsen*, *Seydlitz* managed to take onboard a few hundred tons of desperately needed fuel, and while this was in progress, engineers were transferred onto the tanker to assist in the repairs. Anxious hours later, *Seydlitz* was able to cast off, reposition ahead and take the tanker in tow, now heading south away from the busy shipping lanes. For the next four days, they headed south, the engineers managed to repair two of the boilers by robing parts from the remaining boiler, and although she would be slow, at least she would be able to make progress on her own. *Seydlitz* came alongside, and finally filled her bunkers to the top. Now he could continue his mission.

As they approached the 'Horn of Africa', the starboard lookout on the destroyer *Napier* spotted something strange on the horizon.

"Dhow on the horizon green 80."

"Very good, Potts, there are lots of dhow's around here, what's disturbing you?" the OOW asked.

"She was sailing parallel to use when I first spotted her, but now she has turned a full 180 and is heading away from us, that's odd, sir!"

The OOW knew that Potts was one of the smartest sailors onboard, and if he thought something was odd, he would call it out. Leaning over the speaking tube, "Captain to the bridge," then to the next speaking tube, "Radar – Bridge, get me a plot on the dhow on our starboard side about twenty miles." As the Captain arrived, the OOW quickly passed on the concern.

"Very good, send a signal to the Flagship, let's see what they think. It's obviously not the German 'heavy' we are looking for, but might be something in it"

A few minutes later, the signal arrived '*Napier* investigate!'.

"Hard a-starboard, ring on for thirty knots," the Captain commanded.

In a flurry of foam, and with the 'bone between her teeth', *Napier* sped off in the direction of the dhow. Watching from *Stockport*'s bridge, Matley thought *Napier* looks great at that speed, in the lovely clear blue sea.

As the distance reduced, Potts, looking through his hi-power binoculars spoke up, "They're throwing something overboard, sir!"

The first thought on everybody's mind was 'Mines!'. The Captain spoke, "Pilot, steer a course away from the stern of that dhow, come to ten knots, 'Bunts' signal that dhow to heave too, bosun prepare to launch the seaboat, port side, signal the flagship, tell them what we are doing, and 'Guns' prepare to open fire!"

Potts yelled out, "Oh God, they are people being thrown overboard."

Another lookout yelled, "Confirmed, sir, people!" As the distance reduced between the two vessels, a strange odour drifted across to *Napier*.

The Pilot yelled out, "She's a 'Blackbirder'!"

"Surly not, not in this day and age?" spoke the Captain. As they approached, the awful truth dawned on

Captain Weeks. To the bridge he spoke, "It's a slave ship! Launch a second boat to try and recover those poor devils from the sea, 'Master at Arms', armed boarding party, I want the '*gentlemen*' on that ship in chains ASAP! Bunts signal the flagship, tell them what's going on." In angry frustration, he lashed out his left foot and kicked the bridge coaming!

"She's not stopping, sir," a voice rang out.

"Guns, a shot across her bows, close as you can."

A moment later 'B' gun recoiled back on its springs, a four-point five-inch shell ripped through the air, the familiar smell of cordite drifted across the bridge, and the shell exploded across the dhow's bows, and she started to slow down.

The Captain yelled, "Away seaboats, gun crews keep a close eye on that dhow."

After a tense fifteen minutes wait, the officer in charge of the boarding party waved towards *Napier* that all was well. Weeks allowed *Napier* to approach the slave ship, the smell getting stronger as they closed the gap. He watched as one of his sailors on the dhow rushed to the ship's rail and wretched overboard. 'What had he seen', he thought.

The sun was high in the sky when the Boarding Officer returned to the ship. He looked shocked, and Weeks spoke softly to him, "In your own time, Pilot."

"Yes, sir. She's a slave ship, sir, the '*Muhadi*', out of Suakin in Ethiopia, there are/were two-hundred slaves from East Africa, being transported to Oman for sale. I don't know how long they have been travelling, but they are in a very poor state. There are ten surly Arabs in charge, and nobody is owning up to being the Captain, so I have locked them all in chains in the main hold, let's see how they like it! As far as I can tell, there were fifty-one thrown overboard, but with their chains still on. So they have sunk to the seabed, sorry we couldn't do anything for them."

"OK, thanks, Pilot. Have the crew changed on the dhow, and send food and water over. I will speak to the 'Old Man' and see what is to be done."

After a long conversation with Lee, it was decided that a small steamer party under a 'Subbie' would take the *Muhadi* to Djibouti, hand over the ship and the slaves to the authorities there, and let them deal with it. *Napier*'s sailors would rejoin the ship later.

As they exited the Red Sea, the carriers started launching Avenger search aircraft. The force still doing sixteen knots, once clear of the Horn of Africa, they head southeast in search of their quarry. The Destroyers and Frigates took turns to refuel from *Olna* and *Arndale*, the forces tankers. For four long days, the various search aircraft scoured the sea, but with no sign of the enemy. They received a signal from the Admiralty, which said that a warship had been sighted near Madagascar, so the force headed in a southerly direction. The fifth day brought a slowdown, as they took turns to refuel from the tankers, especially the escorts, but the carriers were also running short of petrol for the aircraft. A Sunderland reported that there was no trace of any warship near Madagascar, so the force spread it searchers in a wider pattern. The force continued deep into the Indian Ocean, with still no sightings. Lee was getting more and more frustrated, where has the raider gone?

The Brothers sat under the Perspex canopy and were lulled into lethargy, going about their jobs with little enthusiasm. The dependable Pratt and Witney engine in their Avenger, *Diane Joyce*, droned on. Hour after hour, they scanned the featureless sea, with little to show for their efforts. John and Peter Carrie were the sons of Lee's Chief Yeoman, and although they should not fly together, they had managed to get themselves assigned to the same aircraft, so after six months, they were a competent flight crew. The third member was back on the ship; out here there was little chance of needing their rear gunner, so he was left behind, which allowed them to take onboard more fuel to extend their patrol. John was the pilot and had a love of flying ever since he was a young boy; planes fascinated him. Peter was the thinker, he excelled at navigation and as his role of observer, he commanded the aircraft, but despite petty squabbles, they worked well as a team. They reached the end of their southern search pattern leg and turned ninety degrees to starboard. This leg would be flown for thirty minutes, then head northeast, home to *Striker*, a bath and bed. They droned on, and directly ahead of them a thin column of smoke appeared on the horizon. John pushed up the throttle, to gain a bit more airspeed, and headed to investigate as Peter quickly worked out their position, and made ready to use the radio.

As they closed the smoke, it became apparent that it was two ships sailing in close proximity, the smoke coming from a decrepit-looking tanker, and alongside was *Seydlitz*!

"Pete, quick as you can, get a message of, 'Found 'em'." As he spoke, red and black cotton wool balls appeared around the aircraft, and the crump of exploding shells could be heard over the drone of the engine. The plink sounded as shrapnel peppered the right side of the fuselage. The pilot turned to port to get out of range and pushed on the throttle, adding maximum boost. The navigator was frantically sending out messages on the radio. Slowly, or so it seemed, the aircraft put distance between itself and the enemy gunfire. Soon they were out of range and John went through his checklists. Pete started checking his position and fuel calculations. Miraculously they were both unhurt, but their beloved *Diane Joyce* was damaged, and the warm smell of hydraulic and engine oil drifted in and out of the cockpit. Most of the instruments showed that all was well, apart from the hydraulic pressure gauge which was flickering up and down, indicating there was an issue. Pete was struggling with the radio; he was having problems getting through the atmospheric conditions to the ship. John was following a course to return to the ship, nursing the damaged Avenger higher to give them more chance of survival. After a short time, the gauge stopped flickering and dropped to zero pressure, the last of the fluid had gone. With no hydraulics, their landing back onboard would be 'interesting', to say the least. Eventually, Pete managed to get through to one of their sister search aircraft, who relayed the message back to

Striker, now they could concentrate on their survival, it was up to others to do the rest.

Chief Yeoman stepped forward, "Message, sir, from *Striker*, 'Found 'em'!" The atmosphere onboard *Stockport* lightened immediately, and smiles all around.

"Thanks, Bunts, when *Striker* is ready, ask for course, speed, direction, and a plan of action." "Captain Matley, would you join me in my day cabin please?" They entered his cabin, just as Timmins laid a fresh pot of coffee on the table. "Timmins, how did you know?" Lee asked.

"Well, sir, there is no point in getting older if you don't learn something!" He smiled and left the cabin. Lee and Matley just smiled.

Two hours later, the carriers turned into the wind and launched the airstrike on the German ships. Above *Striker*, a badly damaged Avenger circled, waiting for the flight deck to be clear. They had managed to lower the undercarriage manually, but the tail hook would not come down, and now unknown to them, the engine had started losing a lot of oil and was getting very hot, and now the airflow had been altered by the lowering of the undercarriage. Finally, the last strike aircraft left the deck, the deck crew raised the safety barrier and stood by their fire equipment, first aid parties at the ready, as John Carrie brought *D.J.* down for a three-point landing. Unfortunately, he misjudged the speed, and the lefthand landing gear hit the flight deck round down; this sheared off as the aircraft slid sideways in a shower of sparks into the safety net, followed by the fire and rescue teams who arrived just as the aircraft came to a rest. Fire axes and crowbars attacked the Perspex canopy as the brothers were unceremoniously dragged from the cockpit. Fortunately, there was little fuel left and the small fire was quickly extinguished. The two crew were quickly dispatched to the sick bay for attention to their minor injuries. Across *Stockport*, an anxious dad looked on with fear in his eyes.

A strike force of thirty Avengers and fifteen Hellcats headed towards *Seydlitz* and *Sachsen*'s position. High above, a circling bomber kept up a steady flow of position reports. All the strike force had to do was follow the radio signals. The end for the Germans came mercifully quick, the fighters streaked down to a low level and strafed the upper decks of both ships, causing untold casualties amongst the exposed gun crews. The bombers, taking deliberate aim, with their mixed loads of torpedoes and five-hundred-pound bombs tore the heart out of the two ships. All at the cost of two fighters and two bombers damaged, one fighter shot down, and the pilot being rescued later.

Ludendorff heard the alarm sound and rushed from his cabin to the flying bridge, he stopped abruptly as he looked skywards! Advancing towards him were dozens of aircraft. Clearly, the aircraft they spotted earlier had managed to get a sighting report out, and although they had thought they had shot it down, these were here seeking revenge! He looked about his command as his men went about their business, gun barrels started to sniff the air as they searched for targets. The sailors, now wearing anti-flash gear and their 'Coal Scuttle' helmets, stood by for action. The 20.3 cm guns barrels, at maximum elevation, could not track the aircraft, so would stand idle and silent for the action to come. Twelve 10.5 cm gun barrels commenced their efforts to protect the ship, closely followed by twelve 3.7 cm AA guns, then lighter weapons as the aircraft came in range. *Sachsen* was ordered to take any action necessary to escape, but at 11 knots, Ludendorff held little chance of her survival. But he needed to save his ship, Putting *Sachsen* at the back of his mind, he started issuing helm orders, as *Seydlitz*, twisted and turned as she attempted to evade her tormentors.

The Hellcats commenced their strafing runs from different directions, their .50 calibre machine guns spreading death and destruction amongst the unprotected upper deck personnel. The first five-hundred-pound bomb hit abreast the aircraft hangar, setting fire to the Arado 196 in the hanger. The bomb then continued through the armoured deck and exploded in the main switch gear room, destroying all the ship's communications. The next bomb was a thousand-pound armoured piercing weapon; this hit the top of turret *Dora* and penetrated down to the turret ring, causing massive damage, but failed to detonate. *Seydlitz* was then struck by a torpedo; this hit just aft of turret *Bruno*, the bulk of the explosion going upwards, destroying the lower part of the bridge structure. A second torpedo hit abreast the forward boiler room; this flooded immediately and caused *Seydlitz* to turn to port. The next hit was another thousand-pound bomb; this also penetrated the massive steel deck and exploded in the main engine room, blowing out a large section of the keel. The ship was doomed, her back broken and all power lost, and she slowly turned in a circle. Captain Ludendorff was hit by a .50 machine gun bullet, and like his ship, he lay on his side, his back broken, a huge hole in his side as his lifeblood ebbed away, his last order was to abandon ship, and he went down with his command.

Sachsen didn't last long, hit by three torpedoes and multiple bombs, she exploded in a huge explosion, and there were few survivors.

Onboard *Stockport*, the sense of relief was very evident. Lee sat in his chair, Matley by his side.

"You know, Alf, not long ago we would have had to close the enemy and stand toe to toe and slug it out with them, now we can sink the enemy two-hundred miles away and never see them. With a few aircraft we can do the same job, but with a lot less casualties amongst our people."

"Yes, sir, it's becoming a different kind of war!"

"Bunts, send a signal to the carriers 'well done and splice the main brace', also tell *Cleopatra*, *Stinger* and *Scorpion* to rescue survivors."

There were about two-hundred survivors from both ships; they were happy to be alive and away from the war. The force headed northwest towards Port 'T', the Royal Navy's secret base at Abbu Atoll in the Indian Ocean. Overhead, the Combat Air Patrol droned on, ever vigilant for enemies. As they passed the boom into the lagoon, the new fuel farm dominated the scene. The tankers headed that way to top up, the escorts headed for the stricken tanker *British Loyalty*, which after being torpedoed by U-183 and had been beached to save her from sinking, she now served as a refuelling jetty. The heat was relentless, it was a happy set of sailors when the ships sailed the next day for the fleet base at Trincomalee.

As they approached the lush paradise of Ceylon, the aircraft had been flown off for routine maintenance, some to *RAF China Bay* and the remainder to *RNAS Lanka*, a naval airbase recently opened near Colombo.

13 The Arakan

The following days for Lee were filled with meetings, conferences, planning, and endless paperwork. So, it was a happy time when he left with a few of his Commanding Officers for the 'The Highlands' at Kandy, for the cooler air and to escape for a few days' rest.

In number 2 seaman's mess, L/S De Asha, Jenkins and a few others, had changed into their white, shore-going uniforms, and were headed up to the quarterdeck ready to take the Liberty Boat across the harbour. De Asha spoke quietly to his 'oppo' Jenkins, "Listen, I keep telling ya, go and see the rating in the 'Slop Chest' cabin, slip him five bob or gulpers or both, he will give you a brand-new uniform set, press 'em good, and with new boots, keep 'em in your ditty box, then, when they Chief turns up for a kit inspection you have freshly pressed uniform ready. You stick your 'every day' and your 'Tiddly' suit in a bag in your 'ammock, no one will know and it means you have more time to yourself." He continued, "an while you're up on the 'office flat', go and see the NAFFI assistant, slip him a few bob and you can get free 'nutty'. You have been to see 'Doris' in the stoker's mess, to provide you with hot water for dhobying, right?"

"Yes, done that hooky," Jenkins replied.

"Good, make a seaman of you yet," chuckled De Asha.

Nipper was on the deck to see them off, his tail wagging furiously, he was the ship's mascot, having been picked up in South Africa after a confrontation with a few locals. He was desperate to go with his messmates, but not this time. It was a happy excited crowd that stood waiting. The Cox'n, called them to attention, ready for inspection by the OOW. Once he was happy with their appearance, after all this was the Flagship, the Cox'n gave the standard address about staying out of trouble, pride in their ship, and keeping away from the local loose women, with dire threats if anybody came back onboard with VD.

Dismissed, they descended to the launch. Then when loaded, it cast off and headed for the jetty. As the men relaxed, the sounds of 'Role out the Barrel' thundered across the anchorage. A flock of Shearwaters (or Ardenna cameipes) rose screeching into the air as the singing disturbed their feeding.

Once ashore, De Asha headed the stampede into town, having been there before he knew all the hot spots. First a ramshackle restaurant for a curry. Then onto the Fleet Canteen for some cold beer. Followed by a visit to the cinema, to watch the latest Spencer Tracey movie. With four hours left, they headed to the 'Red Light' area to find some physical comfort. Then back to the Fleet Canteen for more beer. It was a happy, if inebriated bunch of sailors who boarded the Liberty boat back to the ship. Again, singing the songs that were popular at the time, the launch bumped alongside the boarding ladder. The Chief

Crushers' stern voice rang out over their heads, "Cox'n keep them men quiet, they are not coming onboard my 'war canoe' like that!"

Just outside the town of Kandy, Lee and the rest of the officers were relaxing by the swimming pool. Originally built by the East Indies Company, this Hotel was used by European employees, with tennis courts, Polo ponies, and crochet courts, all free to use during the summer months as a place to escape from the intense heat. All too soon, it was time to return to the ship and the war.

They sailed on the tide, the sun just peeking over the trees of this lush paradise. The obligatory Local Escort Force of Minesweepers heading out first, to check for submarines and mines, the 30th ACS following in a stately fashion. Once they had sea room, the carriers turned into wind to receive their repaired and replacement aircraft. Two additional aircraft also landed; these would be Hellcats fitted with cameras and they could also function as fighters, a splendid addition.

Their first task was to provide ground support for the 14th Army near Mandalay as they were in a desperate hand-to-hand combat with infantry from the 33rd Japanese army. Once clear of land, the aircraft returned to the carriers, the crews rested, and with their replacement and repaired aircraft, they were ready to go again. Destroyers spread out in the usual escort fashion around the carriers and headed northeast into the Bay of Bengal. The Fleet train followed about twenty miles astern. Search aircraft took off, and the CAP took station over the top of the ships. Just before they left the harbour, three RAF officers had come onboard

Striker. They were to coordinate the strike for the Army, again another new invention. One would be aboard a strike aircraft and he would oversee the ordinance delivery.

The following day, they were on the Burmese coast, awaiting orders to launch. Sat in their brand-new Avenger aircraft, *Diane Joyce II*, the Carrie brothers had been chosen as the lead bomber aircraft, and with an RAF liaison officer onboard, they would circle the battlefield, directing the action. With additional radios fitted onboard, there was no room for the TAG, so he had to be left on the ship. *Striker*, along with the rest, turned into the wind and started to launch their aircraft. This was to be a maximum effort, Forty Avengers and thirty Hellcats clawed skywards. Every aircraft was loaded with two-hundred-and-fifty, five-hundred, or thousand-pound high explosive bombs. First on scene, *DJ II*, circled, in radio contact with the troops, and an action plan evolved. The Avengers in line abreast, ten aircraft in each line, would drop their ordnance together as directed by the Liaison officers. The first line rolled in, and on command dropped their deadly cargo across the lush jungle. Minor anti-aircraft fire reached up to try and swat the attacking aircraft. The high explosives rained down on the enemy troops, death and destruction devastated the Japanese side of the battlefield. With the bombers returning now to the carriers to rearm, the Liaison officer directed the Hellcats to dive bomb and strafe specific ground targets. The Army command post called an end to the strike, as units of the 14th Army moved forward through the devastated jungle and captured the enemy positions virtually unopposed. All the aircraft returned to the carriers safely.

After the strike, *Striker*, *Stord* and *Van Galen* remained on station to assist the army, and the rest of the 30th ACS moved south towards Cox's Bazaar. Their orders were to sink or destroy anything of value to the enemy. Following the tried and tested formula they had worked so hard at in the Mediterranean, first a recon flight took place on the night previous, and the main strike hit the port and airfield as dawn broke. Three small trading ships, a schooner, and some barges were sunk in the estuary, and the few obsolete aircraft on the airfield were destroyed. Again, there were no casualties. Moving further south two small warships were spotted tied up at the pier at Dakhinpara; both were old converted trawlers, armed with a small 37mm gun, and minesweeping gear. The Hellcats fighter bombers from *Fencer* made quick work of destroying them; fortunately for the enemy ship's crews, there were a few minor casualties. Further south, the port and airfield at Sittwe, next came under attack. Five 'Betty' bombers were destroyed on the airfield and a small coastal tanker sunk at its moorings in the river. Lee withdrew his force to the middle of the Bay of Bengal to refuel and rearm, and await the return of *Striker* and her escorts.

When they had finished refuelling and were awaiting *Striker*, Lee watched as the barometer dropped like a stone, the sea started to rise, and the sky turned from dark blue to black, a storm was on its way! Soon, it was as dark as night, the wind was howling through the rigging, rain lashed the upperworks, and the seas had risen dramatically. Matley ordered safety lines rigged and access to the upper decks was banned, as the ship battened down for the fury of the storm. The storm hit them with tremendous force. Soon each ship was fighting for its very survival. Waves reached up and crashed across the decks. The carriers emerged as submerged rocks as the seas tumbled from their flight decks. Aircraft, life rafts, ships boats, and deck fittings were all swept overboard by the ferocity of the storm. *Stockport* buried her bow into a huge wave, and the crew hung on as Lee and Matley prayed for her to rise. The noise was tremendous, slowly, very slowly, the bows rose from the sea, as the waves crashed against 'A' and 'B' turrets. It was every man for himself, this was survival! Lee ordered the ships to break formation and fend for themselves. Onboard *Stockport*, a steady string of casualties was reported to the bridge, as men lost their balance and fell onto the unforgiving steel. Still, *Stockport* fought on, the structure of the ship groaned as she was twisted and turned by the force of nature. The list of damaged items started to grow longer. 'Would it ever end?' Matley thought, and prayed hard. For three days, they fought for survival, and as the fourth day dawned the seas started to moderate. Damage and casualty reports started to flow to the flagship, the sun emerged and the deck and upperworks started to steam as the heat from the sun dried them out. Lee received an urgent message from *Stord*; she was in dire need of fuel, and her tanks were nearly empty. He ordered *Olna* to head towards her to refuel.

It took two days to repair what damage they could. Serious damage would have to wait for a dockyard. Eight aircraft had been lost overboard, twenty-eight men had been injured, some seriously, and three men had been lost overboard while trying to tie down an errant aircraft on *Nabob*. They continued south, this time they were entering the Andaman Sea, and back to the war.

But first, they would strike the port of Rangoon. This would be another maximum effort. It was known that there was a strong force of enemy aircraft at the airfield, they had to be taken out first. There was a change in tactics, the bulk of the fighters would attack the aerodrome. Leaving a small CAP over the force, they launched into the dark night.

They caught the enemy flat-footed, enemy aircraft were parked around the perimeter, and for forty minutes, the Hellcats eviscerated the place, aircraft funeral fires littered the whole area, hangers, workshops, and mess huts were all destroyed. This left the strike on the docks free to start. The Avengers then attacked in waves and fell on the undefended docks with a will. As the aircraft delivered their ordinance, they returned to the home carrier, had a quick rearm, and returned to attack. For two hours they ran riot, a Naval auxiliary, along with three 'Emily' flying boats was sunk in the roadstead, four medium-sized freighters, four small freighters, and dozens of lighters and dumb barges were left sunk or sinking, warehouses afire, and a drydock with a small warship was blasted. Also, two second-class Destroyers were left listing and on fire, along with a small naval tanker, hit and run ashore and wrecked.

It was a jubilant set of flyers that returned to the carriers. Unknown, a 'Betty' bomber had followed the strike force back to the carriers and stayed on station to watch where they were going.

The aircrews took a well-earned rest. As the Aircraft handlers went about their business, aircraft were moved down into the hangers for servicing and repairs, and the CAP was changed on a regular two-hour period. The search planes continued with their sorties. In the north, *Diane Joyce II* started her turn to the south, it was time to go home. They were flying at ten thousand feet, there was a heavy cloud bank above them at twelve thousand feet, but below was unlimited visibility. They droned on; three sets of tired eyes scanned the area around them. The TAG, Ian Shaw, passed the last of the lukewarm coffee and the remains of the bully beef sandwiches forward. These were consumed will little enthusiasm. They picked up the homing beacon from *Striker*, range forty-eight miles away, dead ahead.

"Well, Pete, you might be a useless brother, but you certainly know how to navigate!" John chuckled as Pete Carrie threw a balled-up pieces of paper at the back of the pilot's head. Shaw, just sat there shaking his head, 'Here we go again!' he thought. The squabble continued for the next ten minutes, until Shaw had had enough and threatened them with violence when they landed. Suddenly, without any notice, a Japanese bomber emerged from the cloud layer, about five hundred yards in front of them. The red 'Meatballs' clearly visible on its wings.

"Bloody hell, were did he come from," shouted the pilot.

"Ian, get on the radio, tell 'mother' what we have found, and our position." The navigator passed a note, to the TAG, Ian, with their position on it. While this was going on, John climbed the aircraft into the cloud layer to formulate an action plan.

The enemy aircraft was a Mitsubishi G4M naval bomber, with a crew of seven men and a top speed of two-266 mph and endowed with exceptional range. It was clearly stalking the carriers. Their Avenger bomber was slightly faster at 278 mph, and a bit more manoeuvrable, but the Betty was more heavily armed. Clearly, they had to do something about this. It would take too long for the CAP to reach them, and they could not afford for the enemy to keep broadcasting the carrier's position. So, it was agreed that they should engage the enemy. Their priority was to take out the tail gunner, his twenty-millimetre canon was lethal to the Avenger. The Avenger had one machine gun pointing forward and the TAG sat in ball turret with a machine gun at the rear of the cockpit. They both charged their guns, judging their closing speed, as they descended out of the cloud, the enemy was a lot closer, but was alongside them, not in front as they had hoped. The Avenger gunner quickly cranked the turret to the right, and let fly with his machine gun. The fuselage of the 'Betty' lit up with sparkles as the bullets tore through the thin aluminium skin. A row of bullet holes extended from the cockpit aft to the tail gunner. They had caught the Jap bomber completely off guard. Shaw aimed at the waist gunners' position and blasted it, then he traversed left and aimed for the left engine and the cockpit area. The aircraft was in its death throes, the pilot was dead, so the aircraft turned un-commanded into the 'dead' engine, rolled on its back and dived straight into the sea. As it passed the front of the Avenger, John Carrie also gave it a raking with his forward-facing weapon, just to make sure it wouldn't fly again. What a victory and not one single shot fired in return. When they landed back onboard *Striker*, the whole off duty crew lined the ships side and 'vultures' row' to welcome them back. As soon as the aircraft had landed and moved forward into the parking area, the aircraft crew chief appeared with red paint and a brush and applied a Japanese Rising Sun kill marking to the cockpit area of *Diane Joyce II*.

The Betty had done its job well. From two 3rd Army Air Force, airfields in Malaya, a force of Bombers and fighters took off and headed for the 30th ACS position. This was a mixed force of 'Peggy' bombers escorted by 'Frank' fighters. These had only recently arrived from the 'home islands'. They were the latest from the Japanese aircraft factories. The Mitsubishi KI 67 (Peggy) was fast at 350 mph, heavily armed, and could carry bombs or torpedoes. The 'Frank' was Nakajima KI-84 Hayate. The best Japanese fighter produced and was on par with the finest US fighters, in skilled hands it was lethal.

Onboard Mark Beddall's *Ruler*, his radar team had spotted the enemy air force as it lifted above the radar horizon, long before any of the other ships in the 30th ACS. *Ruler* had onboard an experimental radar set, (it had been fitted in Trincomalee) along with three of the specialists in radar technology, that was far superior to the current, in-use radar sets. This gave them an edge; all available fighters had time to get airborne and gain altitude before the enemy struck. The message went out to all the ships, air raid red, so all ships' guns were manned and ready. *Stockport, Diadem*, and *Cleopatra* commenced firing at maximum range, the black and red clouds appearing around the attacking enemy aircraft. One aircraft was seen to emit smoke from an engine and it turned back, the rest droned on. The first batch of Hellcat fighters fell on the bombers, as the 'Franks' dived down to cover their charges. The second and third waves of Hellcats joined in the melee. This was a turning, twisting, gun firing, 'knife fight', with neither side giving quarter. The Allied pilots had had months of combat training first in Norway, then the Mediterranean, and now in the Andaman Sea. They knew their trade. The 'Franks', although brilliant, the aircraft were crewed by inexperienced pilots with one or two experienced flight leaders, did not stand a chance, and they were decimated. Two Hellcats were hit and the pilots had to bail out. Davies, the Senior Pilot, watched in horror as a 'Frank' with vivid fuselage markings, dived down and opened fire with his machine guns on the two helpless pilots. Riddling their bodies and parachutes with gunfire. With pure anger in his heart, Davies jammed the stick forward, opened the engine up and added maximum boost, in a desperate attempt to reach the fast-departing KI-67. It was obvious he could not make up the distance, so in frustration, he fired a five second burst at the departing aircraft, knowing he could not hit it at this range. As he let go of the firing button, from his left a Peggy flew through his bullet stream. Riddled, it went down in flames.

Above and around the carrier force, Hellcats were attacking 'Peggy' bombers. These crews were the best the IJN had, and they knew their trade. The carriers weaved and turned as they dodged bombs and torpedoes; The destroyers circled the force spewing out a thick smoke screen to aid defence. *Diadem* was hit in the bows, she lost the forecastle up to 'B' gun mount in a violent explosion. The *RFA Edna* and the river class frigate *Tyne* were sunk by a combined torpedo and bomb attack, and *Stinger* took a bomb hit on 'X' mounting, causing extensive damage. Six Hellcats and an Avenger were destroyed, parked on the flight deck of *Nabob*.

With the last of the Japanese aircraft disappearing over the horizon, it was time to land on the exhausted fighter pilots and render aid to the damaged ships, count the casualties and replace the ammo lockers, and look after the wounded. It was well after midnight when the 30th ACS resumed is voyage south. Lee retired to his cabin and prayed for his men.

14 Malacca Straights

Lee received orders, he was to attack the Port of Penang, there was good intelligence that three German long-range U-boats were based there, along with four Japanese Cruiser Submarines. At the next refuelling, he called a conference onboard *Stockport*, of all the carrier Captains and their Senior Pilots. As *Nabob* Captain commented, 'Very Nelsonian!' The sea was flat and calm as four launches made their way to the Flagship. The occupants were welcomed aboard warmly by Matley and ushered down to Lee's Day Cabin. Timmins had laid out a meal for everyone, and drinks were available. Lee was an avid nonsmoker so smoking was not allowed in his cabin. After lunch, they cleared the table, and Lee laid out the charts for Penang. They talked for a couple of hours as a plan was thrashed out. What was paramount was the Carriers could not be risked in the Malacca Straits. With limited sea room, this was not a place to be lingering. Again, they would steam at full speed, to just off Georgetown, launch the aircraft, then head at full speed back North. This was again another maximum effort, six aircraft would fly CAP, and the Bombers would strike the docks and drydock and any shipping in the roadstead. Every available fighter was to strike at the old RAF airfield at Butterworth, enemy fighters were not to be allowed to take off! Davies would fly high above the strike and direct his aircraft where needed.

The thundered south at the carrier's maximum speed of sixteen knots. The warm night air flowed across the flight decks as the ground crews did their last checks on the aircraft. Windscreens polished, ammunition boxes dragged across the deck, torpedoes and bombs loaded, and the refuellers finished topping off tanks. At the ungodly hour of 0330, the force turned into the wind, the first aircraft started their take-off run; heavily overloaded they staggered into the warm air, the blue glow from their exhaust visible to anyone who carried to look. One Avenger fired a red flare and returned to land, its engine spluttering and misfiring badly. Soon the six aircraft allocated to protect the fleet were the only ones left. The pilots sat in their planes on cockpit alert, ready to go.

Wave hopping to avoid the enemy radar stations with their searching electronic eye, the force flew on. Twenty miles from Penang, the fighters zoom climbed up to twenty thousand feet. The first rays from the sun peeked over the jungle canopy. The airstrip at Butterworth opened up to them; they could see, sat in dispersals, Franks, Zeros, the odd Willow trainers and a scattering of bombers. Davies and his wingman climbed higher so he could watch the airfield and the port.

The fighters fell on the enemy parked aircraft with glee, 'it was shooting fish in a barrel' as one happy pilot later stated. A few Zero fighters were being prepared for flight, and as the Hellcats tore across the airfield, their guns spitting out death and destruction. The three Zeros never got off the ground, destroyed under a hail of incendiary and high explosive bullets. The anti-aircraft guns opened fire, as allied fighters were chased by exploding 25 mm shells. These gunners were not on par with their German and Italian comrades, this being the very first air raid they had endured. Once the aerial threat had been eliminated, the Avengers could go about their business unmolested. The three U-boats were spotted tied up, in a line, at one of the wharves. One Japanese sub was at the refuelling pier, and the second one was in the floating dry dock having repairs completed. There was no sign of the third and fourth Japanese submarines. 'The Brothers', lead the strike on the three U-boats. In *DJ II* they dived down and laid their four five-hundred-pound bombs directly across the middle boat. This erupted into a huge cloud of debris, smoke and flame, the boat split into two pieces and sank. As they pulled out of the dive, they felt the plane shudder, as a 35 mm shell exploded at the rear, damaging the fin and rudder. Although sluggish, *DJ II* was still airborne; with no rudder control, their direction could only be controlled by using the ailerons and trim tabs, so it was a zigzag course back to the carrier for them. As the strike continued with its deadly business, the fighters joined them, adding to the destruction at the port. With the final bomb, and torpedo exploded behind them, and the aircraft headed home. The bombers had done their job well, two U-boats, *U-235* and *U-778*, were sunk, and *U-974* would never sail again because her damage was too severe. The Japanese Submarine *I-156* was destroyed in the dry dock, its back broken as it was blown off its blocks.

The remaining submarine *I-158* did not sink but had a huge hole blown in her upper casing, another one that would never sail again. Along with numerous small trading vessels, two more minesweepers sunk and an armed Trawler beached and on fire.

To the east of Banda Aceh, cruising along at periscope depth, Lt. Cdr Sumio Tanabe in his Cruiser submarine *I-155*, could not believe his eyes. Emerging from a tropical rain squall, four enemy aircraft carriers had just appeared heading straight towards him. It had been a frustrating patrol so far, with only a seven-thousand-ton three-island freighter and a small local trader for his efforts; his supplies were running low, so he was heading back to his base at Penang, and would again have to listen to the despised Germans submariners on how good they are!

Although currently out of range, he headed on an intercept course, and brought his crew to action stations. This would make the Germans sit up and take notice. Peering again through his attack periscope, he noticed that the carriers had turned and were landing on aircraft; another ten minutes and he would be in range. Ordering a full spread of six type 92 torpedoes from his forward tubes, he also ordered the last two remaining torpedoes loaded into the two stern tubes. Taking relative speed, bearings and distance readings, these were constantly fed into the 'Fruit Machine', an electro, mechanical calculator, which gave him constant readings to help him aim his torpedoes. Its nickname came from its flashing-coloured lights as it crunched the numbers. The machine had come into possession of the IJN when a badly damaged Dutch submarine had been captured. It was immediately recognized as being vastly superior to the equivalent IJN system, so had been quickly copied and installed in Japanese submarines. Now it was grinding out its deadly equations for the enemy. Tanabe watched and waited, taking quick peeks through his 'scope as the carriers came nearer. As two carriers came into view, they overlapped, so giving a longer target to aim at. He fired all his forward tubes, then turned the boat as quickly as he could and aimed the stern tubes at a cruiser, and another carrier, and fired. He then took the submarine deep and increased speed and headed away from the enemy.

The 30th ACS had just cleared a tropical rain squall, and the aircraft started coming back in ones and twos. These were the damaged aircraft, two Avengers firing red flares to signify an injured man onboard. *Nabob* and *Fencer* turned into the wind, the crash barriers were rigged, and with emergency crews standing by, they took onboard their wounded birds. The anti-submarine screen had moved further away to give the carriers more sea room, but the confused waters of the Straits made for poor Asdic operations.

A terrified shout from *Nepal*'s masthead lookout rang out, loud and clear "Torpedo passing astern". The duty watch scrambled to their action stations as the alarm rattlers sounded, the Tannoy burst into life, "Action Stations, Action Stations, Submarine Action." The Captain, Sam Bullock, rushed onto the bridge.

"What have we got, Guns?" he asked.

"Torpedo passed astern, sir. I have changed course to hunt, the ship is at action stations, also have contacted the Flagship."

"Very well, who's manning the 'set'?" he asked.

"L/S Green, sir, the lad who got that German boat off Norway."

"Good, carry on."

The torpedo shout electrified the force. *Fencer* had just landed on the last of her strike fighters, and the CAP was about to land on, the 'Batsman' on the flight deck was frantically 'waving off' the aircraft in the landing circuit. The ship heeled over to port as she turned at speed. *Nabob* was in a difficult position, she was taking onboard a badly damaged bomber, with injured men onboard, and she could not change course until it landed. The first Type 92 torpedo smashed into her steering compartment, taking off the rudder, and the ships propellor. The second torpedo entered the lower hold deck, where it exploded amongst the stores, aircraft repair shops, and the lower switch room. *Nabob* was dead in the water, listing to starboard, and down by the stern. The two torpedoes from the submarine's stern tubes ran straight and true, *HMS Diadem* literally disappeared, hit simultaneously in both her forward and aft magazines, and she disappeared.

Lee was in his sea cabin when the first torpedo sighting was called, and having heard the rain a few minutes ago, he pulled on his watch-keeping coat. He arrived on the bridge when *Diadem* exploded. He stood transfixed, 'Oh my god,' he thought, 'not again'. His mind went back to so many other good ships lost in this damn war.

"Chief Yeoman, tell *Stinger* to help *Diadem*, and tell *Scorpion* to assist *Nabob*," he ordered. Yet again it was *Nepal* and *Van Galen*, his sub-hunting experts, that found the submarine.

I-*155* was heading south as fast as her electric motors would take her. Tanabe, took the sub as deep as he dared, there were lots of coral reefs in this part of the Malacca Straights, so he had to be careful. Through the listening apparatus, they could hear the destroyers as they hunted him. The steady 'pinging' sound was an assault on their senses.

Nepal kept getting an intermittent echo, but with the strong currents and eddies, it was difficult to pinpoint the enemy sub. Even with *Van Galen*'s help, they could not nail the sub down. So out of desperation, they plastered the area with depth charges. If they could not sink it, they would at least give the crew a headache! The destroyers continued for three hours, as the echo slowly disappeared, unable to verify a sinking, Lee ordered them to re-join the squadron.

Onboard I-*155*, Tanabe had 'bottomed' the sub, the depth charges were uncomfortably close, so they sat on the ocean floor, which may give them a chance to survive. One of the attacks by *Nepal* was close. Lights blew out, instruments shattered, leaks appeared in the forward torpedo room, and the engine room, and the aft escape hatch had lifted in its seating, allowing a steady flow of water. The air was becoming foul, and the smell of chlorine gas could be detected. On the surface, they could hear the hunting destroyers as they moved further north and east. After two hours, they could wait no longer; Tanabe ordered the bilge pumps started and the submarine to surface, he also had his deck gun crews on standby, in case they had to fight. As they surfaced, the gun crews tumbled out of the conning tower, and as the Captain had a quick sweep of the horizon, all was clear. He ordered the diesel engines to start. The cough, rumble, and cloud of blue smoke told its own story. Slowly their speed increased as they headed south to find a safe harbour, and the damage could be started to be repaired. Unseen, above them an Avenger bomber, the three-man crew could not believe their eyes, as a submarine surfaced in front of them. The four five-hundred-pound depth charge bombs straddled the submarine and exploded, crushing the tough pressure hull. *Diadem* had been avenged.

Nabob was in a bad way, although not in immediate danger of sinking, her damage was extensive. Holed aft she had no propellor, the prop shaft was distorted, the rudder was missing completely, and the lower hold had been flooded up to the watertight bulkheads. She was down by the stern and hundreds of miles from a friendly harbour. Lee ordered the tanker *Arndale* to take *Nabob* in tow; *Arndale* was nearly empty, so it made sense to send her back to Trinco, towing the badly damaged *Nabob* with *Tay* and *Exe* as escorts, he could then continue with his mission. Fortunately, *Nabob* had five Avengers and six Hellcats still airborne at the time, so these landed on the other carriers. It was a bit tight, but they could use the extra aircraft.

Lee spoke to Naismith, *Nabob*'s Captain, on the TBS. "Hi, Jerry, sorry about this, do you think you can get her back to Trinco?"

"Hello, sir, we will have a damn good job at trying. I have transferred all none essential flight and deck crew to *Arndale*, just in case, and with the extra pumps onboard we should make it."

"OK, Jerry, have a good trip, and we will catch up in Trincomalee. Good luck and God speed."

15 Sumatra

Moving out of the Malacca Straights, now they had plenty of sea room. His next target was the port of Banda Aceh. From his previous action in this area, he knew there was no love lost between the Sumatrans and the Japanese forces. So, he ordered that great care must be taken when attacking target in and around the port and airfield. Civilian casualties were not acceptable. The evening reconnaissance flight reported some small shipping in the port and roadstead, and some transport aircraft on the airfield. The 30th ACS headed west into the night, its flight deck crews going about their business with professional ease.

On the port lookout station, De Asha and Jenkins were talking about their last run ashore and what a good time they had had. Jenkins confessed that soon after coming back onboard, he had found his genitals were red and sore, and didn't know what to do. De Asha rolled his eyes.

"You silly sod, you've got a dose! Tell you what to do, go and see the SBA ask him to sort you out, he owes me a few favours, offer him your tot, or baccy issue, or whatever he needs, but do it quietly, 'cos if the Crushers find out, its 'The Rose Garden' for you and you'll be on a fizzer."

"Thanks, hooky, do it as soon as I come off watch."

"Make sure you do, silly sod." De Asha said. He shook his head and smiled in the darkness.

Lee stood at the rear of the bridge, he wanted to remain in the shadows. The still warm night was disturbed by a cough and rumble, as an aero engine was tested. The swish of the sea and the gentle hum from the engine room fans filled the air. The quiet conversation of two of the lookouts, turning his head slightly, he spotted De Asha and Jenkins deep in conversation. The scrape of a seaboot, and the gentle sway of an ammunition belt as it moved around a gun tub. All sounds he had grown up with and recognised and accepted as part of his world. His mind wandered, his thoughts returned to the nightmare of the last few years when he seemed to be carrying the whole war on his shoulders, so many ships and men lost, he gently started to cry, turned and made his way to his sea cabin. Matley watched him from a distance.

At 0530, the ship went to dawn action stations, an old naval tradition to be ready in case your enemies attack with the rising sun. However, it was far more prevalent in this time of conflict. First, the sound of one aircraft engine could be heard, then quickly a raucous roar rose from the three remaining carriers as they started to launch their deadly weapons of war. Lee had positioned the force only fifty miles from the port, so the time of flight was very short. All too soon, the aerial killers went about their deadly business. *Fencer*'s fighter bombers attacked the airfield from separate directions. Once the aircraft on the ground had been eliminated, the fighters turned their attention to the hangers, workshops, and barracks, all having palm leaf roofs; these were quickly ablaze. With little or no warning, the rest of the strike force fell on the busy port. Soon, the damage was done, as small coasters, junks, trawlers, workboats and barges were sinking or sunk, with only slight damage to a few of the aircraft. As Davies, high above, looked down on the port, he was happy with the results, and while it was only a pinprick in the Japanese war machine, these strikes were starting to mount up, and he was certain that retribution would soon be on its way.

Once all the aircraft were back aboard, Lee ordered the force to head west, deep into the Indian Ocean, to refuel and resupply. Sat in his day cabin, Lee was going through the deck logs and other paperwork for his daily brief for the Admiralty. He could hear Timmins moving around in his pantry, probably making Lee's lunch. A knock on the door and the Marine sentry called out, "Captain, sir!" and Matley stepped over the coaming and into the cabin. Once inside they could dispense with the formalities.

"Hi, Alf, sit down, pink gin?" Lee stood to pour his friend a gin.

"Thanks, sir. I was wondering if I could have word?"

"Of course, Alf, any time. What's on your mind?"

"Well, sir, it's you I am worried about. I've seen you on the bridge late at night, and you looked in some distress, also Timmins has told me he hears you shout out at night, and you are not sleeping too well." A short pause. "Can I help with anything, sir?"

There was a very long pause, as Lee tried to make his mind up about telling his friend what was on his mind.

"Oh, Alf, I send these young men out every day to attack our enemies, and it's becoming harder and harder to do it, this is my second war, and I am tired of brave men and good ships being lost. Remember when we were in the Med the first time, every day we lost someone, and there never seemed an end to it. We have fought the enemy with the weapons 'Their Lordships' felt were good enough, but they weren't, how many good men died because of the cost-cutting done during the interwar years? Good pieces of kit that were refused, all because some politician said we could do without it! Old men, sending young men to war, to fight for something that in the great scheme of things, didn't matter. Why did we declare war on Germany? Because they attacked Poland, right, then why didn't we declare war on Russia, they did exactly the same thing a few days later, yet nothing was said? We are most defiantly pawns in an old man's war." Lee was quite animated by this stage. "Don't get me wrong, I will do whatever I am ordered to do. After all, I am proud of being English and very proud of my country, but I despair at the antics of our leaders, maybe we do need a revolution every few hundred years or so." He sat back and took a long slug of his pink gin.

Matley looked down at the deck. He had not seen his friend so upset for a long time and he did not know how to respond. After a long silence, Timmins stuck his head in the cabin. "'scuse me, sir, I have drawn a bath for you, and a cup of hot kye, then you can have a couple of hours rest,

Captain Matley and I have arranged that you won't be disturbed unless the ship has sunk."

Lee looked at Timmins and Matley, he had guessed correctly, they both knew something was wrong. "Thank you, Timmins, bless the pair of you."

The following day, the force was hove-to as they refuelled, and rearmed and all the other various jobs that a warship needed to do to remain effective. *Olna* was reporting the oil fuel tanks were down to fifty per cent, but aviation fuel was at forty per cent. *Corinder* was reporting less than twenty per cent bombs and torpedoes left, this after all the ships had refuelled and rearmed. While here, Lee ordered an anti-submarine sweep out to one hundred miles, and the hands to have a 'make and mend', also 'hands to bathe'. As he stood on the quarterdeck watching his men skylarking and splashing in the ocean, for the first time in a long time, he smiled. From the bridge wing, Matley watched his friend through a pair of binoculars and also smiled. Good.

All too soon, the day drew to a close, Lee had invited the senior officers to his cabin for afternoon tea. During the meal, a signalman arrived with a top-secret message from the Admiralty. It read, order one, 'To attack and eliminate enemy forces at the airfield at Palembang in The Dutch East Indies. Once the air threat was eliminated, order two, he was to attack the Japanese fleet anchorage at Lingga Roads'. The meal was soon finished as the officers went back to their jobs, and Lee was able to think about the next attack.

At mid-afternoon, the two specially modified Hellcats took off. They had been fitted with cameras in the underside of the fuselage. Although the camera fittings were bulky, the aircraft could still function as fighters when needed. Keary flew one, and his wingman was in the other. Their orders were one high-speed, high-altitude pass from south to north, over the airfield at Palembang, then continue to Lingga Roads, again one high-speed pass, from east to west, then return home, as fast as possible. The time was critical, they had to be clear of the Naval Base at Lingga before the sun set, so their navigational skills needed to be perfect to find the carriers again in the dark. Due to a mix-up on *Ruler*, the photo Hellcats were not ready for launching. They launched twenty-five minutes late, which left Keary with a dilemma; if he continued with the plan, he would arrive over the roadstead after dark, which was pointless, if he increased speed, he would be short of fuel for the flight back to the carrier, if he avoided the 'dogleg' over the Sumatra and go straight to the target, he would save ten minutes. But he could give the position of the carriers away, what to do? As they climbed for height, they put on the oxygen masks and set the aircraft for maximum cruise, climbing to reach the thirty-seven-thousand-foot altitude. Keary then started scribbling on his knee pad, the photo Hellcats were heavier than the other aircraft, so the fuel consumption was greater, distance was an issue, and in the end, it was a no-brainer. No deviation, straight to the airfield at maximum speed, then onto Lingga, if the light held out, then climb for height, and go onto minimum fuel 'burn', they should just make it back. At this height, it was cold; Keary was glad he had put his sheepskin coat and leggings on, they were uncomfortable at lower levels, but up here, perfect. He glanced across at his wingman, Nick Jones, a big rotund lad from the farming stock in Cheshire, but solid and dependable.

Scanning the horizon, Sumatra soon peeked over the horizon. He soon spotted their waypoint, the highest peak, Mount Dempo, as it towered over the jungle. From here it was a straight run north, across the airfield and then onto Lingga. Keeping radio silence, Keary made the signal to nose the aircraft over to increase speed, and to switch on the cameras, nestled in the aircraft's belly. At 400 mph, they streaked across the airfield at thirty-thousand feet, camera shutters clicking away, the secrets below revealed to the two Hellcats. Jones looked in his rear-view mirror just in time to see a line of black explosions behind him, trying to catch up with his speeding plane. Very soon, they were out of range, as they climbed back up to thirty-seven-thousand feet, they turned slightly NNW, to line up with their turning point, the headland at Belangcor. A sharp left-hand turn straight across the anchorage, then home. As they approached the turn point, they nosed over again to thirty-thousand feet and speeded up to 400 mph. The sun just gave enough daylight to take photos, and as they flashed across the warships, the enemy had been alerted, and black and red mushrooms rose to greet them. Underestimating their speed, the bulk of the anti-aircraft shells exploded behind them, except for four five-inch-high explosive shells fired from the cruiser *Takao*, bracketed the two aircraft, both receiving damage. Again, climbing back up to thirty-seven-thousand feet, they could afford to slow down their racing engines to save fuel, they had to get home with their precious photos. Using 'dead reckoning' Keary calculated their course and speed back to 'mother', it was dark and he looked across at Nick. Reflected in the glow from the instrument panel, he could just make out that he was slumped over in his cockpit, the strain on his face very visible, he pressed the transmit button twice, and Jones looked up and gave him a thumbs up, so on they flew into the night. Little did Keary know, but Nick Jones had been hit by a piece of shrapnel from the cruiser *Takao*.

They droned on into the night, Keary watching his wingman closely. It was obvious that Nick was struggling, his head slowly slumping forward, then jerking back. He looked into his cockpit, to check his calculations and his fuel state. When he looked up, Nick was nowhere to be seen; he frantically looked around. He then rolled his aircraft inverted, just in time to see a large explosion on the ground. He returned to the upright, and said a short prayer for his friend, then he calculated the crash position and concentrated on returning to the carrier. The red low-fuel light started to flash; he looked frantically out of the cockpit, searching the darkness for his carrier. The carrier radio beacon suddenly started bleeping in his earphones. Good, he tuned the locator to the carrier, and locked on. He was forty miles away, and turning the fuel mixture down, he eked out the remaining fuel for a few more miles. Suddenly, the night sky lit up as *Ruler* turned on a searchlight and shone it straight up. Keary relaxed a little, he headed for the light, and he also turned on his navigation lights so the carrier could see him. He picked out the turbulence from the ship's wake, and as he lined up to land, the deck landing lights on the carrier sprang into life, and the batsman's tennis bats lit up, an occurrence unknown on a carrier in a war zone. Keary made a perfect landing, and as he cleared the arrester wire, his engine spluttered and died. Made it! The ground crew rushed to unload the camera film from the aircraft's belly cameras, and the crew chief and the rigger helped the struggling Keary to get out of the cockpit. The first thing he did on touching the deck was to have a pee! It had been a long flight. While the film was being processed, Keary, Beddall, and *Ruler*'s Senior Pilot had a long debrief. After a glass of whiskey, Keary climbed into his bunk and had a fitful sleep, while around him the ship went about its business. The photographs were distributed to the other two carriers and *Stockport*, and a strike plan was worked out, as the carriers and their escort headed at maximum speed to the launch position.

Every single airplane was to take part in the operation, only two fighters and the hastily repaired Photo Hellcat were to be kept for the force's aerial protection. *Fencer*'s fighter bombers would lead the strike, they would attack Palembang as dawn broke, hopefully catching the enemy unawares. Thirty minutes later, the rest of the force would set upon the Japanese warships in Lingga Roads. Once the enemy aerial opposition was eliminated, half of *Fencer*'s aircraft would return to cover the carriers, and the other half would join the attack on the warships. At 0330 in the morning, the aircraft carriers turned into the wind and started to launch the aircraft. By now the deck crews were on top of their game, and the whole strike was airborne by 0400. Lee watched as every aircraft clawed skywards. 'How many would return,' he thought. Once the last aircraft disappeared into the night, silence returned to their little area of the sea. Lee sent a message to the three carrier Captains, congratulating them on their efficiency and professionalism. The force carried on at speed, to close the distance for the returning aircraft. The three remaining fighters sat silently on the flight decks, with the pilot in his cockpit waiting, should they be needed. This was the time that Lee worried the most, his pilots were out of sight, and he could not assist them until they returned, so he prowled the deck, talking to the ship's company to ease his tension. Matley again watched from a distance.

Davies, launched at the same time as *Fencer*'s aircraft, accompanied them to the airfield and circled overhead to watch progress. Once satisfied, he would head to join the other strike. Because of the distance involved, his aircraft had been fitted with long-range fuel tanks, which allowed him more time to loiter over the targets. Arriving over Palembang, he was pleased to see the discipline displayed by his pilots, as they went about the business of obliterating the airfield and its aircraft. Happy with the progress, he headed north to join the attack on the warships.

Unnoticed, he was being stalked by the Japanese fighter ace, **Lieutenant Junior Grade** Tetsuzō Iwamoto IJN, also known as *Tiger Tetzo* by his squadron mates. Flying the excellent Nakajima Hayate, or 'Frank' to the allies, he had taken off in the cool air, before dawn, to do an air-test in his brand-new aircraft. Flying northeast over the sea, he tried some aerobatics and test-fired his guns. Once satisfied, he headed back to the airfield at Palembang. As he approached, he noticed smoke rising and explosions on the ground, as aircraft dived and attacked ground targets. He got behind a Hellcat; he assumed that it was an American navy aircraft, but didn't recognise the wing markings. As he lined up his 20 mm cannons, the enemy pilot spotted him, and performed a zoom climb, up and over the top, catching *Tiger* unprepared. They dodged and weaved around the sky for a few minutes before the Hellcat nosed over, added boost, black smoke belching from its exhaust ports, and headed out to sea. 'Damn,' he thought, 'these pilots are good.' Looking around he spotted another Hellcat, smoking badly as it hedge-hopped out to sea. Taking a quick look around, he pitched over and streaked down to get behind the damaged aircraft. He lined it up in his gunsight; the enemy pilot had not noticed him, and squeezed a two-second burst of fire. The 20 mm shells smashed through the left wing, and as the wing broke off, it turned sharply and spun into the ground. That was enemy aircraft 189 kill to his credit. (He eventually ended the war with a total of 202 aircraft destroyed). Climbing away from his kill, *Tiger* looked for another victim. High above, he spotted a lone aircraft heading to the north. He added power and climbed after it. After a long stern chase, he managed to get within gun range, he fired another two-second burst of 20 mm shells, this time one shell exploded in the gun breech of his left-hand wing canon. This caused his aircraft to yaw badly to the left, and he spiralled away towards the ground, only then did the enemy pilot notice him.

Miles was shaking; he knew he had just had a lucky escape, as 20 mm tracer rounds flashed past his cockpit canopy. He instinctively turned to the right and jettisoned his wing tanks. He could see a plane spinning away from him, going down very fast, but as it was no longer a threat, so he let it be, and continued on to join the shipping strike. He was late getting to Lingga, the strike was in full flow, as he circled overhead, he watched as two aerial torpedoes hit a Heavy Cruiser, blowing off her bow, two destroyers were on fire and a battleship smoking badly. A fleet oil tanker was burning and listing, and what looked like a light cruiser bow sticking straight out of the water like an accusing finger. Finally, another Battleship was down by the bow, listing badly to port and surrounded by a growing pool of precious fuel oil. The sky above was covered by exploding anti-aircraft shells. It was so thick, Davies thought, you could have got out of the aircraft and walked over it. Clearly, the strike was over, so he called all aircraft to rendezvous and return to the carriers.

Racing towards the rendezvous spot, the carriers were intent on closing the gap, just in case any aircraft was damaged and needed help. As they sped north, a fleet of Javan fishermen, in their traditional *Begog* fishing boats were right across their path, so some hasty manoeuvres were needed to avoid them. As they pasted, *Napier* and

Nepal slowed down and closed the two biggest fishing boats. Lee had ordered them to see if they had any useful intelligence on the Japanese forces in the area. After a lot of shaking heads, arm waving, packs of Woodbines being passed over, and some fresh rope and canvas, they were able to glean the disposition of the Japanese forces. Apparently, they are stealing as much rice, fish and animals as they can get, as supplies, are not getting through from Japan. The soldier's moral was very low, and they knew that an allied invasion was imminent. Lee smiled when he heard that. "Not for a long time yet," he commented to Matley. Just as they moved away from the fishermen, medical supplies, fresh fruit and vegetables were also passed over. With a wave, the two destroyers cast off and moved away at speed. The fishermen could not believe their luck, the Japanese had been telling them that the Allies would sink their boats and kill them. This act of kindness would put the Royal Navy in a different light. Unbeknown to everybody, onboard a small fishing craft, a native with a small radio, was transmitting to the local garrison. As the ships disappeared over the horizon, they had been spotted and reported.

The three aircraft that had been sitting on alert were launched as the strike aircraft came back; they would provide protection, while some more fighters were refuelled and ammunition bins replaced, ready for any retaliation. The aircraft that were damaged by enemy action landed first, then the fighters and bombers flew aboard. The strike on the Japanese fleet had taken its toll on the aircraft; five Avengers did not return, three were badly shot up, along with six Hellcats lost and two severely damaged. The flight crews that survived the loss of their aircraft landed and were quickly rounded up by the vengeful Japanese soldiers. They died a horrible death at the hands of the Japanese.

This aerial action had taken a massive bite out of the available aircraft; as the carriers and their escort retired at speed to the south, Lee, Matley and SPLOT had a conversation on what to do next.

16 Hurricane!

There were continuing calls from the 14th Army to help with fighting the Japanese, so it was decided to return to Trincomalee to refit and resupply his ships. There was also a report from the Admiralty that a replacement carrier was on its way to make his force back up to four carriers, and some extra destroyers were to join. They headed back north-westwards; the aerial searches were now conducted at a lower tempo. As they headed across the Indian Ocean, a large force of Japanese aircraft, alerted by the radio message, were desperately searching for them.

This was also hurricane season, and yet again as the force progressed, the skies darkened and the barometer dropped like a stone. All flying was soon suspended, and as many aircraft as possible were struck down into the hangers. Ship Captains, band movement on the upper decks, lifelines were rigged, lookouts had safety harnesses attached to their posts. All loose gear had extra lashings added, and all crews were ordered to wear lifebelts until further notice. The storm arrived, the day turned to night, lashing rain struck to ships like gunfire, the wind howled through the rigging, monumental waves towered over the ships, then fell, pounding the superstructures with thousands of tons of seawater, the noise was tremendous.

Onboard *Stockport*, in number 2 mess, it was chaos; several inches of water swilled around the deck. Lockers and hammocks were ripped from their lashings and thrown into the water. Mess plates, fixtures and fitting in a huge pile slide from side to side. The experienced hands had retired to their hammocks, which swayed in rhythm with the ship. The inexperienced just lay or sat around the mess tables retching into any convenient receptacle. De Asha peered over the edge of his hammock and looked with pity on Jenkins, as he heaved his stomach contents, yet again, into the fire bucket. Nipper, oblivious to the carnage in the mess below, slept peacefully across De Asha's legs.

Lee again ordered the ships to break formation and fend for themselves. The second day, was by far the worst. Lee had never experienced weather like this, even on the Murmansk run, notorious for foul weather, didn't compare to this storm. By the fourth day, the crews were exhausted, bruised and battered, the ships had growing lists of storm damage, but the seas had started abating, and the sun started to show. There was no sign of the Carriers; with their high sides they had been forced downwind by a long way, the destroyers fanned out to collect all the missing ships, and bring them back together. After half a day, most of the ships were within sight. However, *Ruler* was missing, As soon as possible, *Striker* launched search aircraft to look for her. A few hours later, she was spotted far to the south. She was listing badly to port and limping along slowly to the north. Lee ordered his force to the south to rendezvous with the stricken carrier.

Early next morning, the limping carrier was spotted, and the force quickly surrounded their struggling squadron mate. *Ruler* had suffered a loss of power, had turned broadside to the sea, and had been swamped by two huge waves. Aircraft had broken free from their lashings and ran amok in the hanger, smashing to smithereens everything in the forward hanger. A small fire was extinguished in the lower power room. The ship's boats were all ripped from their davits and disappeared overboard, the radar mast atop the bridge, lay at a strange angle, the radio mast completely missing, the front of the bridge had been forced backwards, and two 40 mm gun tubs were totally crushed. *Ruler* looked a mess, but despite that, Beddall had put a brand-new ensign on the stump of the mast and was now flying brightly in the breeze. Lee smiled at that. *Cleopatra* and *Fencer* passed additional pumps across to aid the struggling aircraft carrier. Now they could all head for Trincomalee.

Five days later they again entered the lush paradise that was Trincomalee. *Ruler* went straight into the floating dry dock, as the other weather-damaged ships headed for the dockyard and the support ships. The British Pacific Fleet TF 57 support ships had arrived; they also stood by to assist in the damage repairs to the 30th ACS. Within five days, the sound of the native workforce, riveting guns, welding noises and shouting, soon had the ships returned to a pre-weather-damaged state. Three aircraft carriers had just entered the Harbour. The Escort Carrier *HMS Shah*, *HMS Indomitable* and *HMS Unicorn* had arrived. *Shah* was to join his force in place of *Nabob*, *Unicorn* was an aircraft repair ship and was on her way to join the BPF, but on this occasion with *Shah*, they were being used as aircraft ferries, so their hangers and upper decks were packed with brand new Avengers, Hellcats and Corsairs. *Indomitable* was providing fighter protection for the other two. After all the new aircraft had been lightered ashore, *Indomitable* and *Unicorn* left to join the BPF. Lee had smiled as he saw *Indomitable*, the last time he had seen her, she was a listing burning wreck, being pounded by the *Luftwaffe* in the dockyard in Malta. She had survived and made her way eventually to the USA for extensive repairs, and was now back with the fleet.

Shah's Captain came across to *Stockport* to present himself and to renew acquaintances with Lee, having both served on *Caroline* years ago. As *Shah*'s launch tied up at the gangway, her Captain stopped at the top and saluted the quarterdeck. Lee stepped forward and shook his hand as old friends do. "Hello, Captain Carter, welcome aboard, may I introduce Captain Alf Matley." They shook hands and proceeded to Lee's Day cabin. Once in the cabin, they relaxed, Timmins served coffee and sandwiches. "Alf, this is the splendidly named Cdr. Andrew Seymour Darlington Ives Carter, or ASDIC to his friends! The nickname he was given many years ago." All three smiled, Captain Carter smiled at Matley

"It's OK, call me Asdic, everybody does." He laughed. "I think my parents had a vision for me!" Later after a splendid two hours, and slightly wobbly on his legs, Asdic made his way back to his ship.

The following day, all four carriers left harbour to collect their aircraft which had all been moved to RAF China Bay, and to shake the cobwebs out of pilots and ground crew, and get some flight time in. Miles Davies had been sent back to 'Good old Blighty'. His replacement was Mike Keary, who took over as SPLOT. Once Lee was satisfied, they went back to the war. All four carriers headed northeast, as a few strikes had been laid on for the Army who were fighting, a gruelling hand-to-hand combat with the Japanese. The 30th ACS was to give ground support for the next few days to help a major Army offensive. Once clear of land, the Avengers went about their patrols, and the Hellcats took over the aerial defence of the 30th ACS. *HMS Shah* was slightly larger than the other carriers, so her aircraft complement was greater; she now had a total of fifty aircraft onboard. Twenty Avengers, twenty Hellcats, and ten of the brand-new Chance Vought F4U Corsairs. This was a trial to see how the Corsairs stood up to the rigours of working from an Escort Carrier. Initially, they had come with a fearsome reputation and had been rejected by the US Navy. So, they were given to the US Marines, USN land-based squadrons and to the FAA. A famous British Test Pilot, Captain Eric 'Winkle' Brown RN, successfully landed a Corsair on multiple different Aircraft Carriers and proved that it could be landed successfully. Once established in FAA service it proved to be a formidable fighter.

They left their support ships behind in Trinco, and the Carriers positioned themselves in the Bay of Bengal about thirty miles to the west of Rangoon. From here a series of strikes were flown along the banks of the Irrawaddy in support of an army offensive. These strikes were launched to clear the entrenched Japanese from the East bank of the river. Lee and SPLOT had devised a plan where two carriers would provide the strike aircraft. The other two carriers would carry out the anti-submarine and CAP over the force; after two days they would change positions, and this would spread the workload. After one week, the support ships arrived and replenishment could be undertaken. This evolution was carried on for two weeks, by then the British Army had the Japanese in full retreat. The Far East Air Force now had sufficient aircraft and airfields to take over the support role from the Royal Navy. This allowed Lee to continue with his role of striking Japanese shipping.

The next target was any shipping in or near Port Blair in the Andaman Island.

The submarine *HMS Thunderbolt* had been on station for two weeks; the air was foul inside the sub. The smell of diesel, body odour, and cabbage was overpowering; the hull above their heads was dripping condensation onto everything, and the crew was waiting for night to fall so they could surface the boat and get some fresh air. A voice from the Asdic room sang out, "High speed propellors to the southeast, range ten-thousand yards, possible three warships." Dawson, *Thunderbolt*'s young Captain, rushed from his cabin, "Periscope depth, number one." He stuck his head in the sound room, "Dusty, what you got?"

L/S Jack 'Dusty' Miller, pushed the headset away from his right ear, "Sounds like a Heavy Cruiser and a couple of Destroyer's, sir."

"Do you have a heading?"

"Looks like they are heading north, but they are travelling at high speed."

"Thanks," said Dawson. He returned to the control room. "We are at periscope depth, sir."

"Very good, 'up 'scope'." With a gentle hiss, the shiny tube raised from its pit. Dawson made a quick search of the horizon. Satisfied that the area was clear, he concentrated on the warships he saw in the 'scope. The left-hand ship was a *Fubuki* class Destroyer, the other was a *Maikazi* class Destroyer. In the middle was a heavy Cruiser, its huge 'Pagoda' style bridge structure clearly visible. Checking his copy of Janes, he worked out that it was the heavy cruiser, *Tone*. "Down scope, full ahead on the electric motors, course 020 degrees." Dawson thought for a moment, "No 1, Pilot, bring the intelligence folder, and let's have a look at the chart." The three officers, leaned over the map table, wiping away the condensation from the table surface. They were trying to figure out why these warships should be travelling north at such speed. The navigator was flipping through the Intel folder, and something caught his eye. "Sir, the 30th ACS is up north providing support to the army off Rangoon, this looks like a big enough target, to tempt those ships out of Singapore."

"Yes, that would make sense, there is little worthwhile targets otherwise in this area." Dawson thought for a moment. "No 1, surface the boat, Yeoman, make the following signal to the Admiralty copy in 30th ACS."

Thunderbolt rose from the depths. Once the conning tower was clear of the water, Dawson and the lookouts scrambled out of the hatch. Aft, came the roar, as the twin diesels came to life. Above their heads, the signal reached into the ether. The sub headed northeast at her maximum speed of eighteen knots, the sharp bow cleaving through the smooth sea. This would be a race to get within torpedo striking range.

Lee was dozing in his bridge chair, the sea was calm, and the sun warm, with a gentle breeze. The Chief Yeoman, Carrie, stepped close to Lee. "Message, sir, marked urgent."

"Thanks, Bunts." Lee took the 'flimsy' and scanned it, leaping from his chair. "Captain, can you and the Navigator join me in the chart room, please?" Once inside, Lee showed them the signal. 'From *Thunderbolt*, one heavy cruiser, two destroyers heading north at high speed, seventy-five miles northeast of Port Blair, *Thunderbolt* in pursuit.'

"That will be some stern chase for *Thunderbolt*, good luck to them," spoke Matley.

"OK, Pilot give me a course to get us in range, assuming they are heading into the Bay of Bengal, Alf get SPLOT on the TBS and ask him for a strike plan. OK, let's go and sink some Japs!"

Twelve hours later, the 30th ACS were within one hundred miles of the Japanese warships. They increased speed and turned into the wind; it was crucial that they had enough wind over the deck to get the heavily loaded aircraft airborne. Twenty Avengers loaded with Torpedoes, and forty Hellcats loaded with five-hundred-pound armoured piercing bombs, and the ten Corsairs would fly top cover for the strike aircraft. As they came within sight of the enemy warships, the sky filled with exploding AA shells around the aircraft. Ten Avengers turned left and the other ten turned right, they would perform a classical airborne torpedo attack from both sides of the attacking warships. First, twenty Hellcats were to dive on the enemy and carry out a bombing and gun attack to keep the gunners' heads down, the remaining Hellcats would attack the 'Target of opportunity'. Keary looked out of his cockpit, the enemy ships had realized their predicament and had started to zig-zag and make abrupt speed changes, all in an effort to stay safe.

Keary had a look around the horizon to check all was OK, no other enemy in sight. Giving the attack signal, twenty bomb-laden Hellcats dropped a wing in unison and dived down on the Japanese ships. The first ten aircraft made the *Tone* their priority. Anti-aircraft shells exploded around the diving aircraft, yet they still bore on. As they dropped their bombs, the pilots, now unburdened by the weight, re-adjusted their dives and commenced their gun attacks. From all points of the compass, the Hellcats' guns flailed the decks of the cruiser, decking, ships boats, liferafts and unarmoured gun pits were decimated. Armoured piercing bombs straddled the warship, her sides were riddled by shrapnel from the bomb explosions. Two bombs struck the cruiser's flight deck, smashing the three floatplanes stored there. One entered the small hanger and exploded, the other continued through two steel decks and penetrated the highly volatile aircraft petrol stowage. The stern of the ship erupted as the petrol ignited. Yet another bomb penetrated the deck adjacent to number three 8in gun turret, where it exploded and jammed the turret. The final weapon smashed into the base of the bridge structure but failed to explode. However, it entered the main gun battery transmitting station and completely demolished it. This rendered the main 8in guns out of action. The *Tone* had been hit when the rudder was turned to starboard, and it was jammed, as the crew fought below decks in the emergency steering flat to effect repairs. As she turned to starboard, she narrowly missed ramming one of her escorting destroyers. Eventually, the steering engine was uncoupled and she steadied on a straight course. Three twenty-one-inch aerial torpedoes slammed into her side. The *Tone* had been extensively rebuilt and repaired during her active life. As the additional equipment and armour had been added, her displacement had risen, so she now sat much lower in the water than her designers had envisaged. This caused her main armoured belt to be below the waterline, thus not offering much protection. It was here that the three torpedoes struck with devastating effect. Rolling to port, her stern a mass of flames and exploding shells, the Captain ordered his crew to abandon ship. The two destroyers abandoned their orders and turned to assist with the rescue of their shipmates. Once the Emperor's portrait had been placed aboard one of the destroyers, the Captain returned to the bridge of his doomed command and was last seen saluting as he went down with his ship. Once *Tone* was sunk, the entire aerial strike force concentrated on the two destroyers. Their demise came quickly, both sinking within sight of each other. Many hours later a Japanese minesweeper, a converted trawler, was passing through the area and commenced rescue operations. *Thunderbolt* also arrived around the same time, and Dawson was torn between wanting to sink the trawler and leaving them alone to rescue the stranded sailors. Eventually, he crept away unseen, leaving the trawler to go about its business.

On board *Stockport*, Lee watched with satisfaction as the strike force returned. They had lost one Avenger, the crew being rescued unharmed by the Walrus SAR aircraft, and two Avengers and two Hellcats landed with major damage, a nice return for the loss of three enemy ships. Taking advantage of his supply train, he carried out a resupply and refuel, then headed towards Port Blair, their next target.

Once a British Colony, it was invaded by the Japanese in 1942 and was the Headquarters of the local military. However, it had been stripped of its offensive power as the ships and aircraft had been removed further east to bolster other, more important locations. So, when the 30th ACS struck the Port, Phoenix Bay, on that lovely summer's morning, there was little of military value on the airfield or in the port. The attack aircraft destroyed a few armed coasters, the obligatory minesweeper, and an anti-submarine escort, but left the few local ramshackle coasters alone. Lee had given strict instructions that the local population was not to be targeted. A few obsolete aircraft that were found scattered around the airstrip were soon disposed of. Once the aircraft had been recovered, they moved further south.

17 Palembang

Their orders were to make for Darwin, attacking any and all targets of opportunity on the way south, they had to take some of the pressure off the Australian Army that was fighting its way across New Guinea. They struck again at Banda Aceh, but after the last time, there was nothing meaningful left to attack; a few transport aircraft at the airfield, two small coasters and a *Rufe* flying boat in the harbour, and what looked like an army barracks. On the plus side, they suffered no loss of aircraft and only a few bullet holes to be patched up. Lee ordered armed fighter bombers to be loiter over the land as they progressed south, they had instructions to attack anything that looked military. The aircraft roamed far and wide over the Dutch islands. Trains, depots, bridges, oil tanks, military barracks, and small ports, all felt the presence of the 30th ACS as they continued their movement south. After a week of constant aerial activity, Lee was just about to order a change of course to the south, to retire, and replenish his ships.

Keary was flying on a standing patrol about thirty miles to the north of the carriers. He needed some air time; he had been sat behind his desk for days now and needed to get airborne so he could think. When he spotted a formation of aircraft heading in the direction of the strike force He pressed his transmit button and called a warning. He then circled around to their rear so he could report what the enemy force composition was. It comprised of twelve *Peggy* bombers, ten *Judy* bombers, and a handful of mixed fighter aircraft, *Zeros*, *Oscars* and *Franks*.

The warning brought immediate response from the carriers, as each one turned into the wind, started launching its aircraft, and brought additional aircraft up from the hangers and ranged them on the flight decks. The Hellcats and Corsairs roared off the decks, their engines snarling as they clawed to gain some height. Lee looked on with pride in his eyes, at the smooth action being taken on 'his 'carriers. They had come a long way from that first action in Norway.

As Keary neared the fleet, he watched as friendly aircraft climbed up to meet the attackers. He looked at his fuel gauge. 'It was time to join in,' he thought. Giving a nod to his new wingman, he pitched over and dived down on a *Peggy* bomber, which appeared to be leading the enemy formation. The *Peggy* loomed large in his gunsight, when the wings filled the 'Cartwheel', he pressed the 'tit', his fifty cal. Shells tore through the thin aluminium of the enemy fuselage, the bullets crept forward, and when they reached the cockpit, the bomber pitched upwards, and standing on its tail, it fell to earth in a death spiral. After this slashing attack, Keary continued his dive, then commenced a zoom climb to get back above the enemy so he could carry out a head-on attack. Looking to his right, his wingman was still there. Adding maximum boost and throttle he clawed for height. Once high enough, the air around him was full of turning, twisting aircraft, as the newly launched aircraft joined in the fight. Selecting an *Oscar* fighter, he commenced another diving attack, at the maximum range of his guns. The enemy was lining up on another Hellcat, so he squeezed the tit more to distract the enemy pilot than any chance of inflicting damage, as his bullets swept over the *Oscars* cockpit. The enemy pilot realized the danger he was in and dived to his left; Keary and his wingman followed. They now followed a twisting, turning, zooming, diving dogfight, where neither pilot managed to get a killing shot. After ten minutes, the *Oscar* dived away and fled the scene. Keary became aware his low fuel light had come on so, with the sky empty of aircraft, friend or foe, he turned and headed for his carrier, all along his route back, there were small funeral fires, dotted around the sea. He prayed that they were enemy and not friends. He looked down as he flew over a Walrus flying boat, as it taxied up to an upturned aircraft, clearly a Hellcat had been lost. Now, as the adrenalin was leaving his body, he was shaking, and felt tired and sleepy. He struggled to stay awake as he headed home.

From the intelligence that Lt. Vickers and his team had gleaned, these enemy aircraft had come from Palembang airfield, and they were replacement aircraft for the ones that the 30th ACS had destroyed earlier. Lee watched with pride and sadness as his pilots came back to land. He had already issued instructions that a maximum effort strike was to be readied for another attack on Palembang airfield. The reports from his carriers were he had lost four fighters, three Hellcats and a Corsair. Two pilots had been recovered, and also three aircraft were damaged; they would take six hours to repair. He checked his command, he had enough fuel and ammunition remaining for one strike on Palembang. He ordered that for the following morning.

Commodore Lee awoke at three-thirty in the morning. He had had a very bad night, he had slept little, the names and faces of his lost comrades constantly flooded his mind, when his beloved *Preston* sank again, for the umpteenth time, he had to get up. He was exhausted. Timmins stepped into his cabin, a cheery "Coffee, sir," and placed Lee's favourite cup on the desk. "Would you like some breakfast, sir?"

"Maybe later, Timmins, and thank you." He took a sip of his coffee and headed into his bathroom. Timmins headed for his pantry, he had heard his Captain and friend, shout out during the night and had actually sat by the cabin door, just in case he was needed. He also sent a message to the Marine Barracks for Bennett to attend, in case he needed any help. The two friends sat there through the night having a quiet conversation. Lee would never know.

The bath and the coffee had revived him a little, and as he stood at the back of the bridge, awaiting the fore-dawn action stations, he looked around himself, taking in the sights. On his left was De Asha, the Leading Seaman of No 2 mess, a first-rate sailor, excellent gun layer, and the biggest rogue on board, if there was a scam going on onboard, you could guarantee that De Asha was behind it. Next to him was Jenkins; these two had become inseparable, Jenkins had also turned out to be a first-rate sailor, smart, helpful and willing to work. Bent over the Navigation table was Paul Backhouse, the Navigator, shy and thoughtful, but an excellent ship's pilot, his work was always neat and precise. Chief Yeoman, Ian Carrie, had been with him since *Preston*, solid dependable, and always ready with a quick solution for any signal issue. His two sons were across the water on the Carrier *Fencer*, although he had not said anything, Lee knew he worried about them as every father would. Bennett, the Royal Marine, like the rest of the Marines, was intensely loyal; a man who, you would want next to you in any battle, a superb soldier, but like De Asha, with a drink inside him, a menace, he had been promoted and demoted so many times Lee had lost count, and he never did find out how he ended back onboard *Stockport*. Just then, Alf Matley wandered onto the bridge. Alf, his friend, like Lee was a Regular and had been in the navy since he was a boy, survived the sinking of his destroyer in Norway, an accomplished artist, and a confirmed bachelor. He took a quick look at the deck log, checked the compass and direction of travel, he then noticed Lee standing in the shadows. "Hello, sir, didn't see you there."

"It's OK, Alf, I couldn't sleep, so took a turn around the deck."

Matley nodded but said nothing, Timmins had already spoken on the phone. This was a cross-section of 'his men', the good and the bad, but he loved them all.

The plan had been that they would attack Palembang at dawn, but as the time approached for take-off, the wind had died. It's a natural phenomenon that the wind drops at dawn, this is nothing unusual, but from about four o'clock the wind had dropped to nothing, the sea was flat calm, and with the carriers steaming flat out, they could not get enough wind over the deck to get the aircraft airborne. They could use the deck-mounted catapults, but the time needed for that evolution would take way too long. So, with reluctance, he cancelled the strike, and ordered the ships south to gain some sea room and relax the men, and prepare to do it all again tomorrow. The next two days were the same as the 30th ACS sailed in circles around the Indian Ocean, trying to catch a wind.

Unknown to Lee, the Japanese had guessed that the carriers would strike back at Palembang the following day, and had marshalled as many fighters as possible, ready to ambush any British aircraft. But for three days the carriers were struggling to find a wind. On the fourth day, the Japanese ordered the fighters back to their home airfields as they were sorely missed especially in the New Guinea area. Onboard the carriers, with fuel running desperately short, on the fifth day the strike went ahead. The wind increased and during the night, so they launched their aircraft. At dawn, they fell on the airfield, and what remained of the home-based aircraft were decimated as they sat on the ground in their bamboo dispersals. Bombs exploded across the hangers and hard standings, and Hellcats and Corsairs made multi-directional passes, strafing anything of value. One Hellcat was spotted chasing a man down a road on a bicycle, with gunfire! It was unknown what the outcome was. This last iteration of the strike on this airfield was enough, the Japanese abandoned it.

Finally, the ships headed southeast for Darwin. The Avengers were out and about looking for the enemy. A couple of coastal vessels and some armed trawlers were spotted and dispatched with lethal efficiency. As with the last time he entered Darwin, they were hit by a tropical rainstorm. The skies darkened, and the wind got up, and torrential rain fell across the ships. Unlike the last time, the roadstead was protected by a massive boom, guarded by the Boom Defense Vessel *Barwatch*. *Stockport* flashed the obligatory recognition signal, and the boom was opened. As they came up to their berths, as quick as it started, the rain stopped, the skies cleared, the sun came out, and soon clouds of steam was rising from the drying decks and superstructure on the ships. Three familiar faces were there to meet them, Admiral in Charge of Darwin, his Flag Lieutenant, and Captain Theodore Morehouse USN. As soon as *Stockport* dropped anchor, a USN Landing Craft came chugging across the harbour, and stopped by the ship's companionway, and three happy faces appeared above the ship's rail. After due ceremony, Lee stepped forward and shook hands vigorously with the Admiral and Morehouse. Then leading them down to his cabin, the scuttles had been fully opened and wind scoops fitted to keep the cabin cool, they relaxed and chatted away for a few happy hours, as Timmins kept them supplied with drinks and food. They pressed him about what happened after the last visit to Darwin, his actions with the Japanese Cruisers and the attack by the Japanese carriers, that virtually wiped out his last command. Then they got down to business, Lee explained his need for fuel and bombs for the aircraft, and revictualing for his supply ships, and a few days R & R for his crews. All of which came as no surprise as the RN had already passed on his requests.

Later as the Admiral left the ship, he invited all the ships' Captains, first lieutenants, and senior pilots to a meal at Admiralty House later that day. But first, Lee, Matley and Keary had a job to do, so collecting two cases of whiskey, they made their way to the local US airfield. This had grown substantially since his last visit. Once inside the base it was nice to see that Lt Paine USN was still in charge, and at the cost of the two cases of whiskey, replacement Hellcats, Corsairs, and Avengers soon arrived on lighters alongside the carriers, bearing freshly painted British markings. These were quickly craned onboard and stowed out of sight! Later, Lee sat in an overstuffed chair in the wardroom at Admiralty House. After their fabulous meal laid on by the Australian and US navies, they were now relaxing. He looked with pride at his Captains and Officers, as they enjoyed their surroundings, the noise level was getting louder, but most of that was the rain beating down on the tin roofs of the building, Theo sat next to him, and they were having a quiet conversation and relaxing, letting the noise wash over them. They both wished they could stay here and let somebody else fight the damn war. Lee slowly lapsed into sleep, he awoke many hours later, it was daylight, and he was in a bunk at the rear of Admiralty House; somebody had put him to bed! He did however concede he needed the sleep!

18 Timor: Ambush

He received his new orders, they were to sail north, to re-enter the Java Sea, and create as much damage as they could. As they passed Timor, they launched two strikes, one against the port and one against the airfield of Dili. Later that afternoon, the airfield at Batogade was to be struck. Later, it was reported that a small number of Bombers was based there, if true they could not be left intact. The well-practiced tactics were used again. A recon flight in the evening and a dawn strike the following day. While Keary would lead the strike on Dili, 'The Brothers' would lead the bombers onto Batogade.

The still night air was disturbed as the call went out over the carriers, ships Tannoy, 'Call the hands. standby to spot aircraft'. As usual, Lee was up early, and saying a silent prayer for the safety of his aircrew; he watched from *Stockport*'s bridge as the first aircraft coughed and spluttered into life. Then the roar as they accelerated down the flight decks and clawed skywards. For thirty minutes they took off, joined up into formations, and proceeded north. Then silence descended onto the once busy flight decks, as the Chock Heads went about their business re-spotting aircraft, ready for the return of their birds. As the sky lightened, the normal routine commenced, the decks were swept and washed, brass work polished, ropes flayed down, lashings checked, and then the hands were called for breakfast. The galley served the traditional breakfast fare, porridge, snorkers, train smash, and cheesy, eggy, hammy! Lee retired to his cabin for his bacon, eggs, fried bread and fresh coffee, as Timmins waited on him. He had asked the Bo'sun to make a wooden replica of *Preston*'s ship's crest. Now it was completed and he presented it as a gift to Timmins, a thank you for looking after him so well. Timmins was absolutely bowled over by it, and showed everybody onboard his gift, so proud of it, was he.

The Naval aircraft arrived over their objectives as the sun was rising, the port had a few worthwhile targets, a few small coasters, a couple of schooners, and a large armed Trawler; these were quickly dispatched. The strike at the airfield also held few targets, a small number of training aircraft and a couple of old transport aircraft. As the aircraft rendezvoused over Timor, 'The Brothers' spotted movement to the north, a convoy exciting the Makassar Strait. This was too good to miss. So, after returning to the carriers, they made a quick refuel and rearm, and launched again, this time a convoy was the target.

The bombers were led by The Carrie Brothers, with Mike Keary in overall charge. They formed up over the top of the carriers and headed towards the new enemy.

The convoy consisted of two large tankers, three large merchantmen, and a Cargo liner, with an escort of two destroyers and three anti-submarine escorts. Above flew four '*Rufe*' fighters. These were the famed Zero fighters with floats attached, even with the floats they were nimble and fast, in the hands of an experienced pilot they were deadly. Keary detached ten fighters to engage the *Rufes*. The rest of the fighters pitched over and started strafing the enemy warships at low level, killing or maiming the unprotected deck gun crews. The torpedo-carrying Avengers split into two sections and attacked from either beam of the convoy as the bombing Avengers dived on their targets from above. All too soon, the Allied aircraft had completed their deadly work, One tanker was sunk, the second, after being hit by two torpedoes, had beached itself on the Island of Borneo, The Cargo liner had reversed course, increased speed, and escorted by a Destroyer escaped to the north. The three merchant ships had been sunk, as was the other destroyer and all three anti sub escorts. But it had come at a cost, Two of the *Rufes* had engaged the Hellcats in a swirling, zooming dogfight, that eventually ended over the island of Borneo, with the loss of both Japanese aircraft. The two remaining *Rufes* had evaded the fighters and had struck at the bomber section of Avengers. Three Avengers were shot down, and a fourth badly damaged, before the remaining Hellcats managed to shoot down both *Rufe* aircraft. It was a subdued bunch of pilots that landed back on the carriers, after a long day flying.

The 30th ACS retired to the south, to rearm and resupply, then it was eastwards towards the Arafura Sea, then north into the Banda Sea, to attack anything of military value. During the refuelling the force passed through yet another tropical storm, the rain pounded the ships and their crews, this lasted for about an hour, then the sky lightened and the sun came out, and the ships started to dry under the warmth of the sun. The endless launch and recovery of the aircraft continued, as they searched and gathered intelligence on their enemy in and around the Banda Sea. Several large cargo ships and a tanker were caught and destroyed, along with various small warships and coastal traders and the odd schooner. Later intelligence reported, that, they were causing severe shortages in the Japanese forces in the area.

The Japanese high command had decided that the 30th ACS was becoming a serious threat, so a naval force was assembled, and using the remaining precious fuel, a strong force of warships was sent east to sink the carriers.

Following the latest iteration on the port of Ambon, the victorious allied pilots headed south to return to their floating homes. They were jubilant, they had been out here for weeks now, sinking and attacking anything of military value, they were tired and their aircraft were in need of depot-level maintenance. The ships were starting to feel the effects of continued sea duty. Commodore Lee had been in contact with the Admiralty, and it had been decided that they would head to Darwin for R & R, get the aircraft serviced, and the ships refitted. It was a happy bunch of sailors as they headed towards Darwin.

Sailing, from Lingga Roads, and meeting the other ships from Singapore, the Japanese naval force headed east through the Java Sea. Stood on the bridge of his Flagship, Rear Admiral Sumio Suzuki watched his ships through his binoculars, it was a shadow of the former powerful

Cruiser/Destroyer force of the IJN. His Flagship, the heavy cruiser *Kumano*, was powerful, well-built and heavily armed, but she had an engine problem that the Singapore dockyard could not fix, one of her turbines had stripped its blades. So had been shut down awaiting their return to Japan. His other Heavy Cruiser *Furataka* had been bombed by the Americans in the deadly battles around the Solomon Islands, and her aft twin turrets were out of action, again being unable to be repaired at Singapore. So, she too awaited her return to Japan. The light cruiser *Agano* was brand new, so her condition was unknown. Ahead were his four destroyers, *Natsushio*, *Nowaki*, *Maikaze*, and *Kiyoshimo*, spread out in line abreast, about five miles in the lead, fast well-armed, and with a powerful torpedo battery, they would be his strike element. His objective was to catch and sink the British Carrier task force that was causing chaos in the Dutch East Indies. The few remaining aircraft in the area had been given strict instructions to find and report the carrier's position. Suzuki was letting his mind wander; months ago his last command the Cruiser *Kako* had been sunk by a force of British Cruisers and destroyers. He wanted revenge, but he also knew that his previous enemy had fought well, and their gunnery had been excellent, this time he wanted to be victorious. However, he knew that without major air support, he would have to catch the enemy unawares. In the intervening time, after his rescue from his sinking ship, he had been promoted to Rear Admiral and sent to Singapore to command there. He had worked his ships hard, they had to succeed to ease the pressure on the army in the Dutch East Indies.

Two of *Shah*'s Hellcats had been sent out to investigate a reported submarine, seen off the Island of Baber. They cruised at twenty-thousand feet, eyes outside the cockpits looking for any sign of the enemy. They spotted something in the water to the north of the island, so the flight leader dived down to investigate. His wing man remained high above on lookout, but his attention was drawn to his leader as he spiralled down to the sea level.

The 20 mm cannon shells smashed his cockpit and took out the top row of cylinders of his radial engine, but the young Hellcat pilot never knew who shot him down. The Kawanishi N1K Kyofu Navy Fighter Seaplane, commonly called 'George' by the allied pilots, power climbed back up to altitude, as his kill went down in flames. The experienced Japanese Navy Pilot watched the other Hellcat, it had realized the danger and had added a boost and headed at sea level back to the carriers. High above, 'George' stalked him, and soon he spotted the carriers on the horizon, and the either was full of his frantic radio messages.

The superior radar set on *Ruler* had spotted the two aircraft approaching the carriers, the leading aircraft had its IFF switched on, so it was identified as friendly; however, the second, much higher machine was not transmitting any signal. It took a few minutes for the tired operator to realize it was an enemy, by which time the enemy had spotted the carriers. Lee listened to the aerial reports, it was obvious that they had been spotted, and were about to be engaged by their enemy. He ordered a search to the North and West, and additional fighters made ready for launching. There was nothing else he could do for now; he needed the enemy to show its hand.

Exiting the Flores Sea, Suzuki split his force, *Kumano*, his force 'A' with *Maikaze* and *Kiyoshimo* slowed down, he wanted to attack the carriers at night, something the IJN had practiced for years, a nocturnal torpedo attack. The remaining ships, force 'B', headed at speed to the east to catch the enemy in a pincer attack. The faster warships sped off into the distance. Onboard *Kumano*, the crews went about their business, Suzuki let them rest for a few hours, then at 2100 hours, he ordered them to have a meal, noodles and boiled beef, the sailors' favourite, washed down with a glass of the famous Tiger Beer from the stocks in Singapore. Once fed, they changed into clean clothing and made their way to their action stations. The ship's physicians cleared away the mess tables and set up emergency aid posts, laying out their surgical instruments ready for instant usage. The ship settled down to stalk their enemy. Lookouts in the upperworks scanned the far horizon for a sight of the carriers, using their binoculars, with the finest lens in the world. Onboard the rest of the Japanese force, similar preparations were being made. Suzuki made his way to the small Shinto shrine to make a small prayer. The few crew members looked on in awe, as their Admiral prayed. All around the ship, the traditional Hachimacki, appeared on the sailors' heads.

The ships in force 'B' having gone further east, now turned south. Fortunately, it was a moonless night, and the ships were ready for battle. As they headed south, they increased speed, they were working on dead reckoning, and their calculations showed they were a few miles north of where they should be, so they increased speed to close the gap. The area around the ships was punctuated by small rain squalls, which made observations difficult. Suddenly two starshells exploded above their heads, the ships were thrown into stark relief by the intense bright light! The heavy cruiser *Furataka* shuddered as she was hit by armoured piercing shells, the pagoda bridge was hit by two shells, which caused chaos in the steering and navigation map room. A third shell penetrated the portside torpedo mounting, taking out the crew and setting a small fire. Following in line astern, *Agano* was hit by multiple shells, and then a torpedo exploded in her forward boiler room, she slewed out of line, as the fire in the boiler room spread. The next in line was the destroyer *Nowaki*, she also suffered dreadfully, under multiple shell hits, she also fell out of line and started to go down by the bow.

On force A *Kumano*, the starshells spotted in the distance came as a shock. Suzuki scanned the horizon for the culprit. Then *Kumano* gave a mighty shudder, hit by a torpedo, a terrific roar went up, and the smell of burning paint and the stink of cordite filled the air. In the corner of the bridge, Suzuki lay in a heap. The ship shuddered again, they had been hit by another torpedo, the ship was now at a steep angle to starboard, it was obvious the ship was sinking and fast! The First Aid party picked up the

Admiral, and under orders of the Executive officer, carried him to the only lifeboat left intact, and gently laid him in it, along with the Emperor's portrait. With no visible sign of the enemy, the two remaining destroyers closed the wreck of *Kumano* and started rescue operations. As *Maikaze* came alongside the wreck, two more torpedoes slammed into the battered Cruiser, the concussion ripped the side of the destroyer open to the sea, and she quickly sank.

Her work done, the submarine *Thunderbolt* quietly crept away into the darkness.

Onboard *Furataka*, her damage was severe; however, the Captain had spotted her protagonists by the fading light of the starshells. With only two of his forward turrets operational, he ordered them to open fire. The destroyer *Natsushio* played a searchlight on the enemy ship, *Cleopatra* stood out like a white ghost. The first salvo was over, as the *Furataka*'s gunnery officer reset the range and fired again. One 8 inch shell hit the forward turret on *Cleopatra*, and with a loud roar, it disappeared overboard, taking the complete gun crew with it. Before the enemy cruiser disappeared, the searchlight was on *Natsushio*, and it exploded in a shower of sparks and broken glass, as an enemy destroyer's gunfire destroyed it. Yet again, *Furataka* is hit by multiple shells, that devastated her upperworks, and opened the hull up to the sea, this time aft below the useless rear turrets. Leaving the sinking Japanese warships, the British Cruiser force withdrew southwards. The daylight would bring the Avenging aircraft to finish what was started that night.

"Message, sir," Carrie spoke in a quiet voice. "It's important."

"Thanks, Chief Yeoman." He read it twice and said, "Captain, can you join me in the chart room?"

"Alf, it's from the submarine *Tempest*, she has spotted a large force of destroyers and cruisers heading our way, they have just exited the Flores Sea. It looks like they are splitting into two groups."

"Yes, sir, looks like a pincer movement on us, before we leave this area, we can't outrun them. Do you have a plan, sir?" Matley asked.

Lee thought for a moment. "Pilot, can you pass me the secret folder?" For a few moments he flipped through the forest of signals. "Got it," he said in a triumphant voice. "Captain, this is what we will do, first we know *Thunderbolt* is off the island of Moa, if she heads at maximum speed, she can be here by nightfall." He points at a spot on the chart. "Next, we will reverse course, and ourselves, *Cleo*, and all the destroyers, will form a gun line here." Again pointing at a spot on the chart. "If I remember correctly, from my time watching the Nips at practice, they will attack after dark, with those 'Long Lance' torpedoes, then close in and attack with gunfire. If the War Gods are good to us, we will come as a shock to the Japs. At dawn the carriers will launch strike aircraft to finish off anything we missed!" A few minutes later, they sent a signal to *Thunderbolt*, outlining the plan. After which he spoke to his Captains on the TBS, he explained what was going to happen. Clearly, the Carrier Captains were not happy, stripping away their protective warships, and just leaving the Frigates as the only escorts was a great risk, but a risk worth taking. Once satisfied that his Captains knew the plan, *Stockport* and the rest of the force, turned back, and with Battle Ensigns streaming, they headed north. Later as darkness fell, Lee watched the bridge radar repeater, as the two enemy forces advanced southwards. He led his force in a wide sweep to port that brought them within firing range, praying that *Thunderbolt* had made the designated attack position. Now he was satisfied, he ordered his and the Destroyers to launch their torpedoes, and following the ranges given by the Radar sets, aimed and prepared his main weapons.

A moment later, "Open fire" and the night erupted.

19 Darwin

The silence was deafening, the cease-fire gongs had just stopped, the gun crews stood back from their weapons, their chests heaving as they gulped in the fresh air, and the decks were littered with empty brass shell casings, along with the other detritus of war. Paint chips, wood splinters, and pieces of shrapnel lay everywhere. The gun line circled back to the north, with the intention of recommencing the fight. But as dawn was slowly creeping above the horizon, through his binoculars Lee looked with pride, horror and disgust at the carnage his ships had inflicted on the enemy force. Above, his Avenger bombers were attacking the beaten Japanese warships, it was a one-sided engagement.

"Captain Matley, call off the aircraft, there has been enough killing tonight, tell *Savage* and *Stinger* to rescue survivors." Lee knew there would be a few Japanese sailors who would allow themselves to be rescued, but he had to try.

"Chief Yeoman, signal the force, well done, report damage, and splice the main brace!"

The butchers bill came in, *Cleopatra* had fifty-six dead, and forty-two wounded, 'A' and 'Q' turret were out of operation, *Stord* had been hit aft, with 'X' gun destroyed, with twenty-one dead, *Van Galen* had been near missed and shrapnel had peppered her port side, leaving eighteen badly wounded, and finally *Nepal* had been hit on the bridge, Captain Bullock and his entire bridge staff had been wiped out, a Sub lieutenant was the only senior officer left alive, who now took command. The damage to his ships, although serious, in some ways they had been lucky, in so much as the ships could still maintain their speed. Lee retired to his cabin, he needed to be alone to grieve for his lost shipmates. One hour later, Lee was back on the bridge, his force was heading south, repairs were in hand on the damaged ships, ammunition was replaced, and the crews had eaten, above flew a strong force of fighters for protection.

Four hours later, they rendezvous with the rest of the force, and they all headed south for Darwin.

Soon the ships were in a great circle, with the support ships assisting *Cleopatra*, *Van Galen*, *Stord* and *Nepal*. His perennial problem reared its head again, as his destroyers were all reporting low fuel levels, so they were ordered to refuel as soon as they were able, with priority to *Van Galen*, *Stord* and *Nepal*. The signals office was busy deciphering all the 'well-done' messages they had received, and a steady stream of 'flimsies' arrived at Lee's bridge chair. The one message he was glad to see, was the Australians were sending him some Destroyers. The day wore on, and a persistent shadower arrived, a long-range, IJN 'Betty' bomber followed the force south, keeping well out of gun range and retreating as soon as one of the fighters looked like they were heading in his direction. As night began to fall, the radar room called up, "Captain, I have four surface ships heading our way from the southwest, Green 10, speed twenty knots, range forty miles."

Matley stood up and made his way to the bridge radar repeater, "Bunts, make a signal to *Shah*, tell her to get her airborne aircraft to check it out, it should be our Aussie friends on their way here. Messenger, go the Commodore, tell him the Australian destroyers are nearly here."

At midnight, the four Australian Destroyers moved into their allotted escort positions. In the morning, with tired eyes, the exhausted 30th ACS crews looked on the Australian warships. Lee came onto the bridge as the day was breaking, he looked with pride at his command, rusty paint removed by the action of the seas, and the damaged warships showing their scars with pride. Ahead and to either side were the Australian built Tribal class destroyers, *Arunta* and *Bataan*, big powerful destroyers, astern in the escort screen was the *Quiberon* and *Quickmatch*, two Destroyers built for the Royal Navy but handed over to the Australians when newly built. They had earned a formidable reputation, and Lee was very happy to see them all, also, they had been built with increased fuel bunkerage, which hopefully would help with future operations.

Darwin arose over the horizon, and as was normal, every available aircraft was launched, a few circled the force, and the bulk of the aircraft landed at the joint RAAF/USN airfield, for much-needed repairs and upgrades. Yet again, as the battered, but proud 30th ACS entered the roadstead boom at Darwin, another tropical storm lashed the ships. In the shelter at the rear of *Stockport*'s bridge, Matley turned to Lee with a huge grin, and above the tremendous sound of the pouring rain, said, "Seems like every time we come here, it rains!" and they both laughed. Following the instructions from the RAN Pilot, the ships took up their allotted anchorage stations, with the carrier *Ruler*, proceeding to the naval pier, and the tankers making their way to the oiling jetty. Yet again, the Admiral in command of Darwin, and his USN Counterpart made their way out to *Stockport,* this time in a naval launch, its Royal Navy ensign streaming in the wind. The side party already awaiting their arrival in the pouring rain! Lee and Matley stood in the lee of 'Y' turret, avoiding the worst of the tropical storm. As the Australian Admiral climbed the boarding ladder, the Bosun's call rang out, "Pipe still, attention on the upper deck, face to port, Port Admiral Darwin, salute!" over the Tannoy. Once on the upper deck, Lee stepped forward, "Welcome aboard, Admiral." They shook hands. "Come below out of the weather," as he and Matley ushered their guests down to the Commodore's cabin, where Timmins had laid out drinks. Above, the Tannoy sounded the 'Carry On'.

Above them on the boat deck, De Asha and Jenkins were working on the thirty-two feet launch; the rain was streaming down, and they were feeling pretty miserable. De Asha spotted the launch and grabbing Jenkins, they ducked down out of sight. "Watch this," he said, "Here comes Admiral Numpty Nuts, just watch all the bowing and scrapping!" They both started laughing. Their laughter was heard by the Buffer, who glared at them. "Oops," said De Asha.

It was hot and humid in Lee's stateroom, with the scuttles opened, and with the fitted wind scoops. The rudimentary air conditioning was struggling to cool the space down. They sat down as Timmins served the drinks, and the Admiral spoke, "Alan, it's always a pleasure to see you back here, and to listen to your tails of daring do, your command is causing quite a stir amongst the Naval authorities here and in Washington, as well as upsetting the Japs!"

"Thank you, sir"

"Now tell me about your last voyage, leave nothing out, 'Flags', make notes," he barked to his Flag Lieutenant, Smyth.

Captain Morehouse USN sat back in the overstuffed chair and cradling his Scotch Whiskey, he soaked up the conversations and the debrief.

Hours later, it had gone dark, the rain had stopped and the ship's superstructures were drying out in the heat, the cabin had cooled down a lot, and Timmins had served snacks to everybody. The whiskey flowed and everybody in the cabin relaxed. The Admiral stood up, "OK, Lee, I will have to go and send an interim report for 'their Lordships'. Come to the Admiralty House with all your Captains at mid-day tomorrow, we will have lunch, and discuss what's next." With that the party stood up, shook hands and made their way off the ship.

Later Lee retired to his bunk, but could not sleep, the demons were active again that night. Outside his sleeping cabin, Timmins and Bennett sat in a silent vigil.

After breakfast, Lee boarded his launch and headed to the nearest carrier *Striker*; he wanted to go aboard all his command and talk to the ship's companies, and to thank them for their efforts over the last few months. As he bordered Wilkinson's command, *Striker*, he was happy to see all things appeared shipshape, and despite the effects of the weather, the crew had turned too, to paint ships, his visit was unannounced, and was pleased with what he saw. Little did he know that Matley had tipped off the other Captains in advance of Lee's 'surprise visit'! In the two and a half hours he was on *Striker*, he talked to as many of the crew, and a few aircrews, as he could. He singled out the Carrie brothers and had a few words of thanks for their efforts, also he passed them a letter from their father, Lee's Chief Yeoman. After speaking to all the ships company from a raised dias, on the flight deck, he ordered *Striker*'s Captain to 'Splice the Mainbrace', after which he got a huge cheer in appreciation.

Along with *Strikers* Captain, he reboarded his launch and headed towards the Naval Pier and Admiralty House. As they landed at the pier all the other Captains were awaiting his arrival. The Australian Navy had laid on transport, and as they started to board, Lee spotted De Asha and Jenkins, driving past in an Aussie jeep! 'What was those scoundrels up to,' he thought.

De Asha and Jenkins reported to the Buffer, soon after the officers had retired to Lee's cabin, to receive their bollocking for showing disrespect, and were ordered ashore the following morning to collect spares and other equipment, as the rest of the ships company had a 'make and mend'. Which with hindsight was probably not the best punishment. On landing, they made their way to the dock office, to collect the first batch of supplies, using a 'borrowed' jeep, they loaded up, returned to the pier and offloaded the parts on the launch, and then headed off to collect more, the crew in the launch awaited their return. After three trips the launch was full, and it headed back to the ship. This was what De Asha was waiting for! As they left the pier, De Asha spotted the Commodore's launch arriving, and putting his foot down, he headed back to the supply store, loaded what he had come for, and instead of returning to the pier, he headed for the town in a cloud of red dust. Down Allen St. to the Park Hotel, remembering to remove the engine's rotor arm, they entered a pub and ordered their first pints of Aussie beer! A few pints later, Jenkins was feeling the effects of the beer and was slowly sinking down in his chair as the beer took hold. De Asha being a hardened drinker had got into a drinking contest with a bunch of soldiers. By three o'clock, De Asha realized that he was very late, and needed to collect the rest of the ship's stores. However, Jenkins was lying comatose on the floor, unable to walk. Enlisting the help of the Aussie soldiers, they carried Jenkins back to the jeep, where they laid him across the cargo on the back seats. Putting the rotor arm back, he started the vehicle and headed back to the harbour.

His mind was working overtime, he needed an excuse for the delay! Above the sound of the vehicle's engine, he became aware of an aircraft engine noise. Thinking nothing of it, he looked skywards. He didn't recognize the aircraft shapes, how odd. Next, came the sound of machine gun fire, and above his head the shape and sound of exploding Anti-Aircraft shells! They were under attack. A row of 20 mm cannon shells stitched a pattern across the road in front of them, and one smashed into the engine of the jeep, this seized immediately, and it pitched the vehicle forward and into the air, landing upside down in one of the deep drainage ditches. De Asha lay on his back, when he breathed it hurt, he moved his head a little. He could just make out Jenkins lying in a heap, a deep gash in his forehead, and with blood seeping out of it. Around him, lay the contents of the jeep, he could make out the bark of anti-aircraft guns, and the crump of exploding bombs. Dust, earth and smoke reaching for the sky. After a short while he heard the approach of footsteps in the gravel, as Australian Engineers and a first aid party came to their rescue.

Earlier out in the roadstead, *Ruler*'s radar team had picked up a large force of aircraft approaching from the north. They called the bridge, but only a young Sub-Lieutenant was on there. Not knowing what to do, he pressed the alarm buzzer. This was picked up by the rest of the ships in the anchorage, who added to the general alarm. It had the desired effect as all the gun crews were at their weapons, loaded and ready for action.

The Japanese had become very concerned with the destruction that Lee's force was causing in their area of influence. Japanese forces had been on the defensive for months, being attacked on multiple fronts, China, Burma, New Guinea, and the Island-hopping US forces. So, they needed to relieve some of the pressure on their forces.

They had tracked the 30th ACS for the past week, and when they arrived at Darwin, they had put together a plan. This was for every available bombing aircraft in the East Indies, to attack Darwin and the Carrier force.

All of the Carrier's aircraft sat on Darwin's airfield. The Japanese had a field day, they plastered the parking areas, causing huge damage to the stored aircraft. The few USAAF P40s and USN F6Fs that managed to get airborne were completely overwhelmed. Once the airfield had been naturalized, the bombers turned their attention to the anchored ships. The sky over the anchorage erupted as anti-aircraft shells blossomed overhead, and lines of multicoloured balls crisscrossed the sky. The sound was terrific as every weapon in the port opened fire at the Japanese aircraft.

As the last enemy aircraft droned away to the north, the anchorage was in shambles. George Metcalf's *Fencer* was on fire and down by the head. Hit by multiple heavy bombs, the ship was doomed. Dave Wilkinson's *Striker* was listing badly to port, she also would not leave Darwin again. Mark Beddall's *Ruler* had been hit by one armoured piercing bomb, that had gone straight through the ship and had failed to explode. Efficient damage control had saved the ship. Asdic's *Shah* had somehow survived without a scratch. The *RFA Arndale* was ablaze, as fuel from one of her ruptured fuel tanks spilled into the river. Three of the escort ships had suffered from near misses and splinter damage. *Stockport*'s port side was riddled with shrapnel holes from two bombs. Workboats and ship launches scurried around the harbour assisting in rescue operations. From *Arndale*'s burning fuel, a huge black cloud hung over the port. Ambulances rushed around to assist the dead and wounded. There was total devastation on the airfield, as the ground crews fought the fires and moved undamaged aircraft to safety. Lee stood on *Stockport*'s bridge as Matley oversaw the repairs to his ship. He looked around the harbour and his heart sank, his command was devastated.

It took two days to put out the fires, assess the damage, and to make a list of the butcher's bill! Radio messages flew across the ether as the Admiralty made new plans. Fortunately, the death toll was surprisingly light for such a massive action; all told, ninety-seven men were dead and one-hundred-and-ninety-seven men injured, requiring hospital attention, and the rest would be termed 'walking wounded'.

The dead were buried ashore with full military honours as Lee attended every funeral.

Soon orders arrived. *Fencer* and *Striker* were constructive total losses, they rested on the sea bed with just their upperworks showing. Salvage operations were already underway to recover as much useful equipment as possible. *Scorpion* and *Tay* had also sunk, having received significant damage. *Ruler* was having a plate welded over the hole in her hull to make her seaworthy again. The other ships doing as much as they can to make the repairs as needed.

Admiralty's orders were in, *Shah* was needed back in Ceylon to assist with operations in the Arakan area. With enough aircraft that escaped the airfield attack, they were able to put together a scratch force of Avengers, F6Fs and Corsairs. She, along with *Avon* and *Dee*, sailed two days later. Lee made every effort to visit all of the ships and thank them for their efforts. The remaining supply ships, *Olna* and *Corinder* along with two Australian Destroyers were to proceed to Sydney, where they would be resupplied, then sail for Manus in the Admiralty Islands and become part of the Fleet Train for the Far East Fleet, Task Force 57. Once repaired, *Olna* was also to join the other supply ships, in the Fleet Train. The Australian warships were to be returned to the R.A.N. The remaining R.N. warships were to return to the UK, for repair and refits, *Stockport*, *Ruler*, and the surviving escorts.

Eternal Father, strong to save,
Whose arm doth bind the restless wave,
Who bidd'st the mighty Ocean deep, its own appointed limits keep;
O hear us when we cry to thee,
For those in peril on the sea.

30th Aircraft Carrier Sq.

4 a/c *Striker* Cdr Dave Wilkinson RN DSC MiD
   Ruler   Cdr Mark Beddall RN DSC
   Fencer   Cdr George Metcalf RN DSM
   Nabob RCN   Cdr Jeremy Naismith RCNR DSM
   SPLOT   Lt Cdr Miles Davies RNVR DSO,
   Replaced by, Lt Cdr Mike Keary RNVR

Replacement Carrier
   Shah Cdr Andrew Seymour Darlington Ives Carter DSO

                                      (ASDIC for short)

   Bristol/Stockport Alf Matley
   Diadem   Robert Gardiner
   Black Prince   Wilfred Summers
   Cleopatra   John Lenton

   26 DF *Savage*   Fred Bignall
   Stinger   Richard Winter
   Scorpion   Lesley Finch
   Swift   Malcom Bradshaw
   Stord RNo N   Stig Holsman
   Napier   Richard Weeks
   Nepal   Sam Bullock

Van Galen Dutch Johan van Geldir

Replacement Destroyers
Arunta,
Bataan
Quiberon
Quickmatch

FLEET Train
RFA Olna Tanker
RFA Arndale　　　Tanker
RFA Edna Store ship
RFA Corindar Store ship.

River Class Frigates
Tyne
Mersey
Tay,
Exe,
Avon,
Dee

Authors notes

HMS Preston, Bristol and Stockport, and her captain are fictional. The actions you have read in book 1 'In Our Darkest Hour', book 2 'The end of the beginning' and are based on true events. This book is loosely based on actual events late in the WWII conflict. There was a carrier force made up of four escort carriers, but to my knowledge, they only saw limited combat operations in the Far East. So, I have included some of the action reports from the R.N. Fleet Carriers in T.F. 57. Obviously, *they* were not involved in this book, nor were their captains.

The 'Town, Southampton, Colony' class Light Cruisers did exist. They were well-built, fine-looking ships, and the Royal Navy were justifiably proud of them. They served in every ocean in the world with distinction and suffered appalling damage and tragic losses. Of the twenty-one built, six were lost, two others so severely damaged they had to be rebuilt, and many others so badly damaged they barely made it home to a safe port.

The Escort Carriers are also genuine, and some of the flight deck experiences are from a conversation with a departed ex-colleague George, who served on *HMS Fencer*. The carriers, as explained, were built cheap, they were expendable, they were slow, but they did the job they were built for. Being built on Merchant ship hulls, after hostilities ended, many were converted into merchant ships.

Aircraft, the American built Grumman F6F Hellcat fighter along with its stablemate, the Chance Vought F4U Corsair, was thought of by many to be the finest shipborne fighters of WWII, along with their bomber partner, the Grumman Avenger. The Royal Navy's Fleet Air Arm, gladly excepted every single one that they were given, for they were far superior, then anything built in Britain at the time.

The captain, and some of the characters, are genuine, but I have changed the names to protect their identity. In my early work years, I spent a lot of time with ex-Royal Navy Veterans from WWII. It was fascinating and humbling to hear their experiences, good and bad. I did take notes at the time, and put them away for future use, and forgot about them for many years. Unfortunately, they have all 'crossed the bar', and it is with personnel regret that they never got to see this tribute to them. It was much later when I heard of the loss of one of my dearest friends, I decided I wanted these memories to be heard. While the 'Official' history of the events at sea is available in many formats, I wanted the personal experiences recorded, and woven into the story, so the general public could understand the stress, terror, sudden death or maiming, the lack of sleep, that these men had to endure. The single lines of text I have added are their stories, are genuine, and they *did* happen.

For all Royal Navy crews, 'That are still on patrol' RIP.

Glossary

40mm / Bofors – A Swedish Anti-Aircraft weapon
Adrift – Late/Absent from place of duty
Ashore – Going outside the establishment you are living in
Bimble – Walk Bird – Nickname for the embarked aircraft. Bish – The ship's spiritual leader. Blackbirder – Derogatory name for a slave ship, 2500 RN sailors died during their eradication war on the slave trade in 18th and 19th centuries. BPF – The British Pacific Fleet, also known as Task Force 57.
Brass Hat – Any officer with gold braid on the peak of his cap.
Bulkhead – Wall
Call the Hands – Means "Get out of bed" CAP – Combat Air Patrol, fighter aircraft stationed over the carrier force.
Civvies – Civilian clothing Chock head – The slang term for naval airman who handle the aircraft on the flightdeck.

Chum – mate.
Chummy ship – ships that work together

Class Leader – A selected member of your class

Clean Ship/Cleaning Stations – Sweeping/Mopping/Scrubbing - Prepare for Rounds

Clubswinger/Clubs – Physical Training Instructor

CPO/Chief Petty Officer – Addressed as "Chief"
Crushers – Ship's policemen

Daily Dits – Daily Orders

DCT – Director Control Tower, where they aim the guns.

Deck – Floor

Deckhead – Ceiling

Dhobi Dust – Washing Powder

Dhobying – Washing - Usually by hand

Dit – A story or quote usually funny

Divisional Officer – Your "Boss"

Divisions – Formal Parade

Duty Part of the Watch – ratings detailed for additional duties that day

Eytie – slang for an Italian
FAA – Fleet Air Arm
Flimsy – Message pad, for Top Secret 'once only' messages
Gash – Baby or new entrant

Gizit – Freebe or gift.

Gulpers or Sippers – Using your tot of rum ration as payment for goods or as a thank you for services rendered.

Goffa – Drink

Guzz – Devonport/Plymouth

H.A. – High Angle weapon used for firing at aircraft.

Heads – Toilets

HMS – His Majesty's Ship

HMIS – His Majesty's Indian Ship

HMCS – His Majesty's Canadian Ship

HMAS – His Majesty's Australian ship.

'Hooky' – Leading Seaman, Leader of a messdeck.

IJN – Imperial Japanese Navy.

IFF – Identification, Friend or Foe. Radio signal transmitted by aircraft to identify them as friendly

Jabs – Vaccinations etc

Jabo – Russian slang word for German Fighter Bombers.

Jack Dustys – Supply Chain Logistician

Janes – World famous authority on ship recognition

Jap – Slang for a Japanese.

Jerry/Nazi/ Kraut – Slang for a German.

Junior Rates – Term for Leading Hands and below

Killick/Leading Hand – Addressed as Leader, Leading Hand or Hooky
Kit Muster – Formal Inspection of your kit
Kye – A thick gluttonous drink made from a block of chocolate and condensed milk. Karavoskaros – Small coastal trading ships L.E.F. – Local Escort Force
Make-n-mend – Afternoon off Marine Barracks – The name for the Royal Marines mess deck.
Matelot (Pronounced MATLOW) – A Sailor/Naval Rating *Maat* – German Corporal
Mess/Messdeck – Living quarters
Muster – Collect/gather at a specific location NAFFI – Navy, Army and Air Force Institutes. Provides luxury, and essential supplies to service men. One NAFFI store on every ship or base.
Nine o'clockers – Later evening meal
No 1/Jimmy – First Lieutenant or Executive Officer
Nozzer – New entrant Nutty – chocolate *Obermaat* – Sergeant
Oerlikon – A Swiss-made automatic 20 mm anti-aircraft weapon.
Oggin – The sea/water

Onboard – Inside the establishment
OOD – Officer of the day
OOW – Officer of the watch
Oppo – Close friend
Parade Drill – Marching and saluting etc
Pipe down – Lights out, go to sleep
Pit – Bed
PO/Petty Officer – Addressed as "PO"
Pom-Pom – 2 pounder anti-aircraft weapon, gets its name from the sound it makes when firing.
Pompey – Portsmouth
Pongo – slang for soldier
Putty – the shore, ship on the putty, run aground.
Rig of the day – Uniform as specified to be worn
Rounds – Formal inspection of your messdeck/toilets/bathrooms
Run ashore – Leisure time down to town
Scran – A Meal
Sea dust – Salt
Secure – Stop work
Senior Rates – Term for Warrant Officers, Chiefs and Petty Officers
Slide – Butter or margarine Slop Chest – The ship's clothing store. SNAFU – Situation Normal All F++ked Up.

Snorkers – A Sausage
Stand easy – Short tea break but also a drill order
Stokers/Clankies – The men who attend the ship's boilers
Supper – Early evening meal TAG – Telegraphist Air Gunner TBS – Talk Between Ships, a first generation radio telephone.
Pusser/Pussers – Absolutely anything issued by the Royal Navy.
Turn to – Start work U.S.S. – United States Ship. Vp Boat – German Auxiliary patrol boat, generally a converted Trawler.
WAFU – (Wet and Fu++ing Useless)
Wet – Any beverage hot or cold
WO/Warrant Officer – Addressed as "Sir"

Japanese warship names

Agano, (Japanese Light Cruisers were also named after rivers (Kawa), but shortened for use on ships, so Agano would have been Aganokawa.

Kumano and Furataka, (Japanese Heavy Cruisers were named after Mountains and Rivers).

Kumano, named after the mountain, Mount Kumano.

Furataka was named after the river. So it would have been Furutakakawa.

Destroyers were named mostly after winds, or weather phenomena:
Natsushio; Summer Tide.
Nowaki; Autumn Gale
Maikaze; Dancing Wind
Kiyoshimo; Clear Frost.